Brick City

By Kariem

Brick City is a work of fiction. Names, characters, places and incidents are the product of the author's imagination or are used fictitiously. Any resemblance to actual events, locales, or persons, living or dead, is entirely coincidental.

BRICKS4Life Publishing
2 Keer Avenue
#3
Newark, N.J, 07112

Editor: Chyna S.
Visit us at www.bricks4lifepublishing.com
Facebook page:
https://www.facebook.com/BRICKS4LifePublishing/?hc_locatio
n=ufi

ISBN-13: 978-0692029411
ISBN-10: 0692029419

Library of Congress Control Number: 2014950861

Manufactured in the United States of America

Author's Note

Blessings and respect; from a person who writes to express to his reader's awareness, pain, freedom, love, and happiness. My goal and hope for writing are to touch someone's life that is hurting. To change the direction of anyone's life that is on a negative path. Hope to become a productive part of society and a part of the solution.

My spirit tells me you will not regret reading this novel. I love and thank you for your support.

Newark is the party capital of Jersey. Places like Shaneek's, Doc's, Zanzibar, New Experience, Club America, Mr. West, Symphony Hall, The Millennium, and Shadow. That would get the dance floors on fire, at one time. Just to name a few.

You are about to enter the 'Bricks' baby, Heavy Hitters! Do not attempt any of this at home. This book is totally fiction. Any reference or similarities to actual events, real people living, dead, or to real locales are only intended to show realness to the novel.

The similarity of names, characters, places or incidents are entirely coincidental.

Enjoy!

Acknowledgement

I must give honor to GOD, which all my help comes from. All praises due to him! With GOD I realize I am so blessed. He gives me a sense of belonging, worth and competence; by allowing me to see the spiritual impact you can give by touching the lives of others!

To all my 'BRICKCITY' people, I thank you for all your love and support.

All my book readers, thank you.

To my wonderful mother (SNOOK) Thelma there is no way I could repay you for all you do, I love you Ma!

To the coolest pops "Mack" Levi, I'm your twin! Endy your help, love, and support is priceless. You are so loved.

My sister Applesauzz (SMH) I guess I don't have to fire you anymore! She named me Charlie from Charlie Angels because I always have the crew of Angels on a mission: Rose, Toni, Lori, Wanda, Kalara, and Dionne.

Shout-out to all my other sisters Tonia, Alexus, Lafonda, Tricee, and Vickie. I love y'all.

Kim and Angela you women are just outstanding. Nothing will ever break our bond, much love.

Sheon I finally finished. You keep me going your love is priceless. Love you, Ms. Madison.

Aunt Gert, thanks for always showing me the love of a mom to her son. I love you.

My Latrise I am so proud of you! I love you.

My Goddaughter Shelly A. Love you, honey.

Linda Andrews see your cuz work! Lol, love you. Lolesha, you're so sweet! Mamma "Hak" love you!

Dimry M. I'm proud of you family! Lamar A. Do your thing, nephew.

Tina and Cheryl, thanks for all your love. Now help me sell some books on Long Island and Delaware, lol.

Anitra, Pete, Latrise, Papa Joe, and Darren, I am asking all of you to forgive me of my many wrongs and not being a better man. I am sincere when I say I love all of you very much! Linda C. God put the right people in your life, thank you for the many prayers and love.

Jan JB; we have shown people that color don't matter when you share a bond of love. You will always be my brother. I love your country ass!

Sgt. Major Michael Mack, job well done cuz. Now help sell some books, Lol.

Big Kayson H. My brother-in-law you stood with me no matter how things looked! For that, you earned the utmost respect. Love you family.

To my brothers Big Rick, Clark, Malik, Elias, Mark, Bain, Rodney, and Jigger, love you all. These men help me by being who they were in my life; Wilson Mack; Uncle Sonny, Uncle Bobby Mack, Theo, Raheem Long, James Isaac. Big Na'eem, Hakim and Will Dixon, Omar (Smiley), D-Bo, Paul, Rich, Hamid, Roshelle, Fat Man, Omar (Poochie) Sharif Fulton, Lil Mahamm, Wali, Tariq Ward, Bruce Sampson, Shaheed Williams, Clarence G., "Puddin'" The Legend, and Greg Sykes (RIP) thank you. Jamal (Randy Williams) R.I.P, and Jamal (Little Dave).

I salute all the men and women that protect and serve our country!

Robert W. Keep Right On Trucking; Keep up the good work cuz!

To all the men and women fighting inside the unfair judicial system of injustice in America, fighting in the struggle allows you to see firsthand how the system will do whatever it takes for a conviction! Stand firm, giving up is never an Option! Rehabilitate yourself, build your mind, and change for the betterment of self. It's time to break the chain. May the peace of God be with you and support you.

To all the family, Mack's, Isaac's, Gregg's, Small's, Andrew's, Grayer's, Ward's, Garner's, Johnson's, Mc Kenneth's, Webb's, Longs, Jackson's, Grier's, Greens, and Dixon's

Last but surely not the least, Ba' you've loved me when I didn't know how to love. The way you showed unconditional love and put up with my B.S! Your faith in God knew that He had control of everything. I could never repay you for being such a great Queen love you and thanks!

R.I. P: My nephew Kayson, I love you, I miss you, and I talk to you every day. Your name is a tattooed on my arm. I know God love you and you are in the best hands, love unc!

Patrick (Pat) you are always my partner forever. Our bond can never be broken, respect, enough said.

My brother down in Jamaica, nuf respect!

Kareem Ward (SC) I love you lil cuz.

Patricia (Pat) W. The FBI couldn't even get you to separate your love from me. You loved your Kariem and I love my Pat! RIP baby!

Cookie, I can feel your smile just thinking of you. I love you, moms!

Inez, you love me so much and I love you. You are always my heart you are my angel and mother-in-law.

Uncle Son, Bobby, and Buffalo love you guys. RIP.

To the women that hold such a blessed spirit whom I had the pleasure of being around, Barbra and Virginia (Welch, and Hester) Sarah Fearrington, and Mrs. Ruby Jenkins you all have touched my life in so many ways real love never fades away!

Aunt Ree, Aunt D.D, Aunt Dorothy, Aunt Lou, Aunt Betty I know God's angels are with each of you.

Hijrah (Hottie) Ward love you always your family!

Whitney Houston, we love you! Your voice will always live inside your city "Newark, Brick City"

To the guys at Lee County Correctional that keep it gully, keep your head up.

For the ones not named they are loved also and my prayers are with them daily. GOD BLESS!

CHAPTER 1

5'oclock in the afternoon on a Saturday the sun beamed on the bricks of Newark, New Jersey. In the summer, basketball stayed jumping at Green Acres.

"What's the Business," Na'eem asked Kaleem.

"Nothin' much," Kaleem responded, "What it do bruh?"

"Where the hell were you at?" Na'eem asked.

"I didn't know we had a game today." Kaleem was late and missed the whole basketball game.

"Man, we needed you; they had two fast point guards that ran all day long. Then Lil Dave won't be back from Africa until next month," stated Na'eem.

"Yeah, that's right, he is supporting that food for Africa program," Kaleem replied.

"Next month when we play 'Surprise' we need our whole team... Hold on, there's Wali." Na'eem said, and then yelled, "Yo' Wali!"

"Look who just showed up," Wali said, gesturing to Kaleem.

"I heard you got off Big Wali," Kaleem said, trying to turn the tables from himself.

"You just have yo' lil' ass in place next month when we play 'Surprise', a lot of money is ridin' on that game," Wali stated.

"Yo', I was going downtown to see the cheerleader showdown kick off, but it was canceled," Kaleem said.

Everybody knew none of those girls could top, when Tiny single handily ripped them apart with her no hand cimmy, landing in the split," Na'eem responded.

"Ouch, that sounds like it hurt," Wali replied.

They all laughed.

"Only if you tried it," Na'eem said.

Na'eem changed into a fresh all white Phat Farm sweat suit and a pair of white on white Jordan's. Music bumped as a black Escalade pulled up and blew the horn… It was Hakim and Omar; Hakim knew his truck was a head turner with new 26-inch Diablo chrome rims.

"What's the business?" Hakim said as the window rolled down, speaking to a few of the guys outstanding around.

Omar stayed in the boxing gym all day on Saturdays so it was a bonus to see him. His hand speed and power punished some of the best in the ring.

"Peace fella's, I'm out," Na'eem said as he jumped into Hakim's Escalade.

"Don't stunt on being at that game, Kaleem," Wali said.

"I'm on it fam, don't trip. I'ma show up and show out!"

"I hear you, I'ma get at you later Kaleem."

"That's what it is, later Wali!" Kaleem stated as they departed.

B-ball goes hard in Newark. Your game had to be tight if you are going to make a statement out there. That meant you had to go hard in the paint. Anytime your team name ring bells, your name will ring as well.

Kaleem felt he had to be at the next game when they play 'Surprise'. With Na'eem being his role model and mentor, he can't let him down.

KARIEM

* * *

Dike is Na'eem big brother. Now, Dike is smooth, laid back, and takes no shit. Dike is black as ever, a handsome pimp. He had women all over Newark, New York, Philly and D.C. Dike never wore sneakers, only wearing five hundred dollars or better shoes, lizards, snakeskin, or crocks. Only suits from Gucci, Yves Saint Laurent, Armani, and Louis Vuitton. He always had four women by his side. They pampered him like a baby, washing him, feedings him, and clothing him day after day. Top model lookin' chicks!

Every time Dike would see Kaleem he would ask the same question, "Kaleem, when I die and retire, you know what I am going to do?"

"No, Dike tell ya' boy." Kaleem would always respond.

"I'm going to start this shit all over again." Dike would tell him.

"One day, one day, I will have a Mont Blanc card and someone will be telling my story, when I die." Kaleem thought.

Depression had taken a hold on Kaleem. Lookin' over his life and not having nothing to show for it. He was a twenty-four-year-old black man living in the hood. The most money he ever saw was three thousand dollars and that was from a car accident he was in on Central Avenue and Eighth Street. With that, his mom's used it to take care of them. He was occasionally plagued by the feeling of not having and wanting to get it. He always wished the money from an armored truck would fly out and he would scoop it up. *Yeah, right!*

It was every man for himself in the Jungle. Who has ever been able to control the Jungle of 'Brick City'? Gibson, James, or Booker? *I don't think so.* Brick City kept their weight up. Kaleem just didn't have anything to add to it.

Some cats that's from the Dirty-South with Hood Justice Entertainment blew through the airwaves this summer. Lo, the Don brought on rappers Money Caliber, Mega-Mills, and a cat named Trigger. Trigger is fire; he would give it to anybody in the industry. All the money that's in the music business… Kaleem just couldn't rap or sing.

Kaleem was always optimistic; he thought, one day he would have Sheik Mohammed Hussein Al-Moudi, Bill Gates, Oprah, and Aliko Dangoto as friends. Maybe even open up a Maserati or Bentley dealer on Route 46 selling cars to Tony and Paulie of the Sopranos. As they would admire his style and swag, demand to see the owner about how good of a salesperson he was. Only to find out that Kaleem is the owner.

Kaleem wanted to make a difference around Newark. By making sure, everyone has a chance to apply himself or herself and not be hinder just because where they live. Their environment nor social media would determine who they are or will be… He thought of having a program called, 'Moving towards Success'. *One day, one day, all eyes would be on him.* One thing for sure, no one could ever take his dreams away from him, no one. Kaleem had only two grand to his name. *That wasn't shit!*

Zeee, Zeee… Kaleem's phone started vibrating. "Hello," he answered after looking at the caller ID.

"Kaleem?" a voice came through the receiver.

[4]

"Yeah, What's good, Pat?" Kaleem replied.

"You need to meet me at University Hospital! Your mom had to be rushed there about an hour ago. Her blood pressure was low and she passed out!"

"What? Is she alright?"

"I don't know. I'm on my way there now!"

"Okay, I'm on my way!" Kaleem responded hysterically and then hung up the line.

* * *

Kaleem ran every light that turned red. Once he made it to the hospital and in the parking lot, he turned into the first available parking space that he saw. He ran through the parking lot straight to and through the automatic doors.

"Hello, can I help you?" the receptionist asked as he approached the desk.

"Yes, my mom's was brought here about an hour ago."

"What's her name?"

Kaleem stood there in a daze…

"Excuse me, sir, what's your mother's name?"

He came out his daze, "I'm sorry, Fatisha Ward."

"Give me a second," she said as she looked at the computer screen. "Who are you to Ms. Ward?" she asked.

"I'm her son," Kaleem responded irritably.

"Okay, Ms. Ward is on the 3rd floor room 304," she stated handing him a sticky visitor pass with the information to the floor of his destination on it.

Kaleem took the visitor pass, stuck it to his shirt, and headed to the elevators. His heart and mind were racing. Once in the elevator, it seemed like everything was moving in slow motion. The elevator doors slowly opened at the third floor. Kaleem stood there for a second before realizing it was his stop and then got off the elevator.

"Excuse me; I'm here to see Ms. Ward," Kaleem stated to the receptionist at the desk on the third floor.

"Sir, Ms. Ward is still being seen by the doctors. Can I ask you to wait in the waiting room? I will come get you once it is ok."

"Damn!" he said as he went to sit down.

Twenty minutes had passed by while he sat there in deep thought.

"Hi, Kaleem," his auntie Pat spoke as she walked into the waiting area where he was sitting.

"Hi, Auntie Pat. I came as soon as I could; had to get those kids together."

"What did they say?" she asked.

"Nothing yet, they said they would come and let me know when I can see her!"

"I had told her she needed to get her rest, going to school and working ain't no joke," Pat stated.

"Mr. Ward, the nurse said you can go see Ms. Ward now. She is still a little under the medication."

"Alright, thank you."

"Hi, ma," Kaleem spoke as he entered the room, hoping when she heard his voice she would open her eyes, *no response.*

"Hi, my sister," Pat said.

Still no response,

"This has to be a dream and tomorrow everything will be just fine." Kaleem thought.

"You know your mother loves you very much. She worries about you a lot being in them streets!" his aunt told him.

"Aunt Pat, I am going to make it out the Brick City jungle of Newark, this is not the life I want to live."

"I see black and whites living and eating good. This dollar-to-dollar shit just can't do it. So if it's the drug game that will make it happen; I will be like "Nike" and Just Do It."

"I hear you loud and clear, Kaleem. You are your own man. My job is to love you no matter what. Many people fall victim to the drug game chasing that mighty dollar. The color plays a major factor in this world today. Still, we have some white people see the same way we do." Pat continued, "Lincoln was the President that won the civil war and abolish slavery in 1863. He had many critics, but that didn't stop him. I recall Grandma Thelma, telling us that many people from the south moved north for better lives. And that South Carolina was the last state to stop slavery!"

"I'm goin' to make it out the hood! You know we were raised in the Jungle of Scudder Holmes projects, eight apartment buildings, thirteen floors, and two hundred apartments inside each building." he said, and went on, "Now check this out let's say that every family has at least two kids. That's thirty-two hundred kids in one hood. Now that's Afghanistan's battlefield…"

"Excuse me, I'm Dr. Hopkins, are you the family to Ms. Ward?" the doctor entered the room and said.

"Yes, we are. I am her son."

"I'm her sister." they both spoke.

"Please to meet the both of you. Allow me to explain Ms. Ward's condition. She was rushed to the emergency room today due to her low blood pressure level. She has been diagnosed with colorectal cancer and diabetes. I want to run a few more tests on her also," he explains.

"Doc, what does all that mean?" Kaleem asked.

"It means that her health is a major factor at this point and time of her life. African American women are at high risk and with early detections; we can attempt to keep the cancer under control."

"We appreciate all your help, Dr. Hopkins," Pat said.

"Yeah, Doc, I'm saying that's my mom's, please do whatever you can."

"My staff and I can promise you that sir. I will keep you up to date on her status."

"Thanks again, Doctor. You have a good night." Pat stated.

"No problem, you guys have a good night too." the Doctor said before leaving out the room.

Just then, Kaleem's attention turned to the nurse that had come into the room… Talking about God's gift, she was light skin complexion, with brown hair and green eyes, large breast, with her backside pushing through her nurse pants, looked very nice. She had to be about one hundred and forty pounds, with a smile that lit up the room.

"Hello." she said, "I'm sorry, but visiting hours are over."

"Hello, yes, we are going to leave now," Pat said.

Her beauty had Kaleem stuck. *"Damn!"* he said to himself, watching her as she checked the machines his mother was hooked up to.

"May I ask your name?" Kaleem asked, and then went on to say, "Since you will be helping my mother, I feel we should be on good terms."

"I'm sorry; my name is Ms. Mack, and yours?"

"Kaleem and this is my Aunt Pat."

"Please to meet the both of you. You two have a good night."

"Good night." they both responded.

"She is beautiful, isn't she, Kaleem?" Pat said as they walked to the elevator.

"Yes, with no ring on her finger." they both laughed, and continued on their way out the hospital.

* * *

"Thank you for the ride, Kaleem," Pat said as he pulled on Howard Street to drop her off.

"You know it ain't nothing. I'm about to make a run to New York with Ta'Rod,"

"Please be careful Kaleem."

"I will, I will," he responded.

"I will see you at the hospital tomorrow," she said.

"Fo' sho', I love you, auntie."

"Love you too, honey."

* * *

Kaleem drove up Springfield Avenue to Ta'Rods house in Irvington on Ellis Avenue. As he rode passed Twentieth Street, many people were standing around in front of the Superior Barber Shop. He honked his horn and kept it moving. He saw Ta'Rod coming off his porch, he pulled over, and Ta'Rod jumped right on in…

"What's up, little man?" Ta'Rod said, gesturing to Kaleem.

"Who the hell you talking to?" Kaleem replied.

"Yo' ass the smallest guy in the car!"

"Ha, ha, ha, not if I put yo' ass out,"

"Ok, you made your point, let's roll," Ta'Rod replied.

As they pushed off, Ta'Rod lit a blunt that he had rolled, and they headed off to the city. Leaving off Westside Hwy, they jumped to 162nd and Amsterdam Avenue, in New York. When they pulled up the block was packed. People were everywhere, Dominicans and Cubans mostly. They found a park, hopped out, and headed into the apartment building.

"Yo', you straight, Pope?" a guy asked as they walked through.

"I got the best coke, trust me," another dude said.

"Check my shit out for free Jersey," yelled another guy.

As they kept it moving into the apartment building and made it up to the third floor, a door opened and they walked inside.

"Capsa, Jersey," one guy said.

Two other guys searched them for weapons. All three of them were armed. A red light sat on the table to signal if the cops were coming to raid. When the light comes on, it meant for them to climb out the window onto a rope that would lead them into the apartments on the second floor, until the raid was over and everything was all clear. Two piles of cocaine sat on the table; the Columbian flakes cost six bucks more per gram, but it was the best coke around at that time.

"What's good Santos?" Ta'Rod asked the man in charge.

"Nothin', Jersey! Who's ya' boy?" ask Santos.

"He's my partner, Kaleem."

"What's up, Kaleen?" he said, not pronouncing his name right.

"Nothin', boss, how you?"

"You know, I like the sound of that, Kaleen," he said with a smile on his face pronouncing the name wrong again. "What you need this time, Jersey?"

"Make it two and a half ounces," Ta'Rod responded.

Santos puts the coke on the triple beam scale, while the other guy counted the money. They were speaking in Spanish. One word Kaleem did know was dinero, "money."

"Good business, my friend," Santos said.

"You too, Kaleen,"

"Ok, boss," Kaleem, replied as they were leaving.

"That joker can't talk for shit, but makes that money, though!"

Kaleem and Ta'Rod headed over the bridge to Newark.

"How is Fatisha?" Ta'Rod asked.

"They have her on a lot of medication. I'm worried about her, man,"

"Everything will be just fine, you worry too much,"

"You know how close mom's and I are and the relationship we share. She is my best friend."

"I feel you, homie, I feel you."

They pulled up on Ellis Avenue back to Ta'Rods place. "I'll be ready to go back in two days no more than three."

"I hope ya' slow ass be ready this time." Ta'Rod barked.

"I will, I'ma get at you later, Ta'Rod."

"Okay, that's what it is, later."

Kaleem wanted to bag up and get some rest, so he headed over to his Aunt Pat's house. During the ride over, he thought to himself, *"It will get better one day..."*

* * *

Knock, Knock, Knock,

"Who the hell is that?" It was six a.m. Kaleem has been sleeping his ass off. "Who is it?" Kaleem yelled.

"It's me, Dawg, open the door. What's good son?" Dawg said when the door opened.

"Shit, I fell asleep,"

"Man, I was getting that money all night and ran out. Shit been jumpin', word. You tryin' to eat?"

"And you know that. I'll be down in a few. Take these packs until I come,"

"That's what it is fam,"

"Aight, I'll see you when I get down," Kaleem stated closing the door behind Dawg.

Just as Dawg said, crazy flow, money coming from left to right. How many, how many, twenties, fifties, and hundredths that were all morning long. It was only 10:00 a.m. and Kaleem sold his whole ounce broke down. *Ta'Rod can't say shit now.*

CHAPTER 2

Later that afternoon, Kaleem still had his mother's nurse on his mind. He arrived at the hospital to find Pat and Ta'Rod were already up there talking as always. His mother had a smile on her face that produced such a glow; it was like a ray of sunshine.

"There is my baby," she softly said.

"I love you, Ma," Kaleem responded, giving her a hug, trying his best not to disturb any of the IVs running to her arms.

"Hi, honey," said Pat as Kaleem gave her a hug.

"You see, he does listen sometimes," his mother stated, and then said, "I always instill the importance of a hug to my son."

"Yes, ma'am," Kaleem responded, and then looked to Ta'Rod, "What's up Ta'Rod?"

"Chillin',"

"You know you keep some good smelling cologne on Kaleem," Pat said.

"Thank you, auntie. Gotta smell good, you never know."

"Never know what?" asked Fatisha.

"Chill, Ma," Kaleem said, giving a little laugh.

"You taught me to smell good too, Kaleem," said Ta'Rod. "You know I had to check ya moms out, after all, I love her also."

"You are too sweet, Ta'Rod," moms replied with a smile, and continued, "I hold all of you in my prayers. I know the both of you are in those streets. I won't judge you because that's not my job to do."

"Ma, not the pep talk right now," Kaleem said, as in, here we go again... Kaleem couldn't wait to tell Ta'Rod that he sold out in a day. Now just wasn't the time to do that.

"You must not stress yourself Fatisha," Pat said. "The kids said to tell you hello and they love you."

"Tell them I love them as well."

Right then a 'Star' walked into the room. "Hello everyone," said Nurse Ms. Mack.

This woman's style and class had electricity running through Kaleem's body. His emotions were running wild for a woman he didn't even know.

"Is it Mrs. or Ms. Mack?" Ta'Rod asked.

"It's, Ms. Mack," she answered.

"Mine is, Ta'Rod." he stated holding out a hand to shake hers.

Her hair was pinned up, but you could tell that it fell below her bra-strap when let down. She knew Ta'Rod and Kaleem were checking her out.

"Another job well did God," Kaleem said to himself.

"Feeling better today, Ms. Ward?" the Nurse asked.

"I do honey, I am," Fatisha replied.

"That's good to hear,"

Just as Ms. Mack was about to leave the room, "Can you stay a few minutes, I'm about to say a prayer?"

"I sure will anything for a lovely patient like you, Ms. Ward."

"Ok, if everyone is ready, let us pray," They all bowed their heads in silence, and Fatisha continued, "Father God, which are in heaven, I thank you for all you have done and will do. I thank you for blessing me with the love of my family and friends. For my Nurse Ms. Mack, which is a blessing as well. Please bless my sister Pat and her kids. Bless Ta'Rod and his family. Keep Kaleem safe and give him direction, so that he may be a productive part of society. Be with the brothers and sisters that are locked down and in hospitals. Be with the young children because they are the future. Thank you for forgiving us of all our sins. I pray these things in your name, Amen."

"Amen to that," Pat agreed.

"Amen." said Ms. Mack.

"Thank you, Ms. Ward, for that beautiful prayer." the nurse agreed.

Fatisha went on to say; "We have so much to be thankful for how about all the people that made a difference in the world today like Harriet Tubman, Nat Turner, Angela Davis, Black Panthers, Tuskegee Airmen and so much more. What happens is America wants us to forget about what Martin Luther King, Malcolm X, Nelson Mandela, Rosa Parks, Emit Till, Assata Shakur, Jackie Robinson and all the political prisoners they still hold today,"

"Over four hundred years of slavery, what should a man do when he can't feed his family?" Kaleem injected.

"That's right," Ta'Rod added.

"Wait a minute, guys," Ms. Mack started, "so many times people chase that almighty dollar like a person on drugs. They have an addiction just for material gain. They have no other purpose. When they die go to jail or are killed it just don't balance out. The media is the most powerful enemy of the earth. But they tend to push aside the racial profiling, poverty, crooked politicians, the bad police with their gangs that are licensed to kill people. Look at Africa our motherland, the second biggest continent in the world, with the biggest production of gold, oil, and diamonds– has the biggest murder rate in the world. This brings pain to us all."

"I understand pain, very well," Kaleem replied.

"I have to make my rounds on the floor. It has been good building with all of you. Thank you for the beautiful prayer, Ms. Ward." After she said her goodbye's she left out the room.

"Ma, hurry up out this place,"

"In Gods time son, in God's time,"

"We about to leave Ma,"

"I love you, Kaleem."

"I love you more."

"You take care of yourself, girl," Pat said.

"I have to, if I don't, who else will?"

"I know that's right," Pat agreed.

"Anything you need just let me know," Ta'Rod stated.

"Okay, all of you please be safe."

They all gave her hugs and said their goodbye's.

As they were leaving, they saw people gathered at the nurse's station. "Excuse me! May I have a moment of your time?" Kaleem stopped Ms. Mack and asked.

"Sure, how can I help you?"

"Ms. Mack, I want to express my appreciation for you taking care of my mother."

"No need I love my job, and your moms is a wonderful person."

"I would like to take you to dinner sometime soon if that's alright with you."

"Thank you for the invitation, but I am much too busy with my work schedule, Kaleem."

"See, they paging me, as we..."

Her name floated through the hospital intercoms...

"Have a blessed day. Don't forget the conversation inside your mother's room." She stated and then walked off, leaving him standing there numb with thoughts going through his head, *"Damn! That woman has the complete package, man, that's exactly what I want in a lady."*

Everyone had plans after leaving the hospital...

"I'll see you two later. I have to go to Pathmark and buy some food," Pat said.

"That's what it is, we love you," Kaleem replied, and they parted ways.

* * *

Back over the bridge once again they go. The George Washington Bridge had to know them as much as they went to New York. Santos had let the competition know he didn't play. Once a guy tried to rob him inside the apartment, Santos had a guy in the closet with an AR-15 that pumped five slugs into the guy's body. Then they cut the body into pieces and fed him as food to animal shelters.

"Qué pasa, my good friend?" Again, his English was broken.

"What's good," Ta'Rod and Kaleem both replied.

"What you need, mi amigo?"

"Four ounces a piece," Ta'Rod answered.

"No problem. Tony arreglar eso para los chicos, mientras hablo con, Kaleen," Santos told tony in Spanish still pronouncing his name wrong. Telling him to fix up what they came for, while he go and talks to Kaleem.

"Come in the back with me my friend," he told Kaleem fanning his hand, gesturing to follow him.

"Damn. What the hell for?" Kaleem thought. "Sure, what's good, boss?" Kaleem's heart started racing.

"You like money, no?"

"Fo' sho', boss,"

"You have more cocaine more money, si!"

"Hell yeah, it's just my stacks ain't right yet when I get right, I'ma spend wit' cha' boss, word."

"I like you Kaleen, give me ya' number," he said pulling out his phone. Kaleem gave him the number and he locked it in.

"I'll be in touch," Santos said.

"That's what it is, boss." Santos extended out a hand to shake Kaleem's before walking out.

"Ta'Rod, you good?" Kaleem asked as he walked from out the back.

"Yeah, we straight; we out, holla' at you soon Santos," Ta'Rod stated.

"Ok, ok."

Santos and his men watched Kaleem and Ta'Rod as they walked to their car. "What was that all about," Ta'Rod asked.

"Oh yeah, Santos talkin' like he may give me some work. I'm not sure, but he got my number."

"That's what's up. We need his ass," Ta'Rod said.

As they were riding back over to Brick City Ta'Rod began, "Yo' back to what that fine ass nurse at the hospital was kickin'."

"Just like Rodney King showed that the truth doesn't even matter anymore."

"You can beat my ass on camera; four of y'all and get found not guilty," Ta'Rod stated.

"Only in freakin' America," Kaleem added, and then agreed, "That was some bullshit."

"How about Nelson Mandela locked up for 27 years, before they let him out of prison in Africa for standin' up for what he believed in." Kaleem continued, "Then you got these street jokers that have made major cash. I mean cakin' in the game done turned snitch. Where the fuck they do that at? When you're true to the game snitching is never an option! Money, Power, Respect 'cause cash rule everything around me cream get the money, dollar, dollar bill y'all, feel me?"

"I do homie," Ta'Rod jumped in. "The system has these old judges that were Klu Klux Klan members back in the day. Now they hold you captive and then kill you mentally or physically. You hear me, Kaleem?"

"Loud and clear my dude."

"Alright man, I will get at you later," Kaleem said to Ta'Rod as he dropped him off at his spot.

* * *

At the hospital the next day, walking down the hallway, Kaleem spotted Ms. Mack coming out another patient's room.

"Hello, Kaleem,"

"Hey, how are you today Ms. Mack?" he responded.

"I'm Fine, thanks."

He spoke and kept it moving to his mother's room trying to keep his composure. He didn't want her to think he was stalking her. *"I damn sure want to do some things to her,"* he thought to himself.

"Hello, my beautiful mother," he greeted as he walked in her room.

"How are you, baby?"

"I'm ready to take you home,"

"When the time is right baby— Kaleem let me tell you something, you know mama won't be around forever and I ask the Lord to keep you covered, son. I have done my best to raise you the best I could. Not all of our days were sunny, but the Lord brought us through many storms."

"I know, Ma,"

"I want you to find your place in life, son. You must always feel good about all you do and have a purpose in life. Don't believe the devil, he will say, you will never amount to anything; you are just like your father. Don't let him trick you son!"

"Ma, I know things will be just fine."

"Excuse me," Nurse Mack said as she entered the room. "I'm sorry; I have to check your vital signs again."

"Will you check mine as well? I know my heart rate has surely gone up."

"Ms. Ward, your son has a way with words."

"Yes, he does!"

"Can you tell me your first name, Ms. Mack?"

"It is Queen,"

"Queen," he repeated.

"Yes, Queen," she replied.

"That sure fits you," he stated, admiring her beauty.

"Thank you, Kaleem. Oh, Kaleem before you leave please see Dr. Hopkins, he would like to speak to you concerning your mom's operation." Nurse Mack stated after finishing Fatisha's vitals.

"I sure will. I'll see you later, Ms. Mack."

"Okay, honey, she replied."

"Ma, I'll get at you tomorrow, I see your MEDs are making you drowsy, and you're falling asleep."

"Okay, son see you later, I love you."

"Love you to Ma." He kissed her on the forehead and left out.

"There is the Dr. by the Nurse's station." Nurse Mack stated, pointing in the direction of the Nurse's station.

"Hi Doc,"

"Hello, Ms. Ward's son right?"

"Yes, how are you doc?"

"Fine, I just want to go over a few things… your mom's heart is not supplying the proper amount of blood that she needs. We want her to be strong enough for surgery. She has a great spirit and we want to do it within the next month, depending on her body. We have the best staff in the state, so that speaks for itself. We always give 100 percent,"

"Doc, I appreciate all of you,"

"Thank you, no problem sir. That is why we are here. Now do you have any questions?"

"No."

"Okay, I'll talk to you later."

"Goodbye, Ms. Mack!"

"Goodbye, Kaleem." she said smiling.

"Oh, before I forget, I have a basketball game comin' up and I would like for you to come."

"Can you play?" she asked.

"Of course, I can play."

"That's what they all say."

"Well, I guess you would have to see for yourself."

"Maybe, we will see."

"Well, that was a good sign, she didn't say no." he thought.

CHAPTER 3

Ta'Rod and Kaleem got an apartment in Maple Gardens in Irvington; which you could cross a few blocks and be back in Newark. Building ten, Maple Gardens was a low-key spot. Ta'Rod was wide open with spending and girls. Kaleem and Ta'Rod were both dressed and ready to go to Club Garage in NYC. The club was always jumping, off the hook with women. In the summer, they would let you party on the roof.

They had blunts rolled, a pint of Cognac, and a six-pack of Heineken. They rode to the club feeling no pain and feeling good. They pulled up to the club, found a park, and finished off the Henny before getting out the car. After the last bit of the Henny was gone, they locked up the car and headed towards the club.

"Damn that line is long as hell!" Kaleem stated. "Ta'Rod, give me fifty dollars."

"You got money, hell nah!"

"I guess you waitin' in line then. I'ma pay off security so we won't have to stay in line."

"Why you ain't just say that," Ta'Rod spat. "Get that pen out the glove box and ya' money joker."

"Here you go big guy," Kaleem said to the security guard when he came back from the car. He passed him a hundred dollar bill and walked off. Kaleem kept his eye on him, when he put the money in his pocket that was their signal to go in.

"Let's roll," he told Ta'Rod. Immediately, they walked right into the club with no problem.

"Nothing but hot honeys, all colors, shapes, and sizes. The Big Apple is lookin' delicious tonight... and you wanted to wait in line." Kaleem told Ta'Rod as they made their way to the bar.

"Can I help you?" asked the barmaid.

"First off, what's your name, beautiful?" Kaleem asked flirtatiously.

"Eva. What you need?" she answered and then asked with a smile.

Kaleem had to get his attention off Eva's C-Cup's jumping out of her tank top. She was sure to get tipped all night.

"Yes, Eva, this is Ta'Rod, and I'm Kaleem and we need two double shots of Henny no ice, and two bottles of Heineken."

"That will be sixty-five, Pope," she responded. Everybody's "Pope" to these Spanish chicks.

"Here is a yard honey... Keep the change. I will make eye contact when I need a refill."

"I got you, Pope." she answered and then carried on to the next patron waiting.

"Ta'Rod, you see honey with her ass cheeks jumpin' out them white shorts? These chicks in here will have our necks hurtin' lookin' at them all night."

"You know I agree, said Ta'Rod."

"Yo' homie! Ain't that the girl from Plainfield?"

"Kaleem, I'm high as hell. How in the hell can I see her? Go see."

"Say no more."

As Stevie Wonder's classic *'All I Do'* bumped through the sound system, she worked her body as she danced on the dance floor.

"Ole' girl is right," Kaleem, said lustfully not taking his eyes off her. "She should belong to 'Brick City' cause she is a brick house." He was on her.

She was about, 36-24-36 a hundred and fifty pounds, light skin, brown hair, and a neck full of gold. She had it going on. All her curves were out there looking right. Even the women were checking her out as well. She knew she had what it took to get a man's attention.

Kaleem walked over and tapped her on the shoulder. "What's up?" he spoke when she turned around and made eye contact. Her hand waved, hello. She was into the song never missing a beat.

"What's your name?" Kaleem asked.

"Diaz." she replied. The smell of her perfume had Kaleem wanting to be all over her.

"Are you from Plainfield?" he asked.

"How did you know that?" she inquired.

"I hit a few clubs in Newark you and ya' girls were at."

She turned her back to him and continued to dance. Her movements said; let me show him what I'm working with. She started rolling her hips, His manhood became brick hard pressing on her, and her ass was soft as cotton. All that she was doing was enough to make a man bust on himself. She spent back around, gets closer to him, and put her arms around his neck. Her breast pushed against his chest. She put her leg in between his, still rocking to the music.

"This nigga holding like the Feds, he got my panties wet." Diaz thought. "What is your name?" she asked.

"Daddy," he answered.

"Daddy?"

"I see you learn quickly." They both laughed.

"Nah, its Kaleem sweetie,"

He knew she felt his meat pressing against her; she had been teasing him the whole record. "Listen, Diaz, check this, I'ma holla' back at you before you bounce, it's a lot of guys tryin' to bark at you."

"Why you worried 'bout them, you scared? Mr. Brick City!"

"Never that, I get down for my crown… feel me? I need that phone number later on, though," he stated, kissed her on her cheek and smiled.

"I'll see 'bout that!" she replied.

Kaleem made his way back to the bar near Ta'Rod. "Yo', that was her man."

"She was throwin' that ass to you out there!"

"Only if she can work the sheets like that," Kaleem responded.

The barmaid Eva was having words with two other girls at the bar that had to be hating on her. Eva was big boned, about six feet, one sixty with a natural golden tan. Eva just brushed the dirt off her shoulder and came over to where Ta'Rod and Kaleem were standing.

"You ready to order now?" she asked.

"Same thing Ma," Kaleem told her.

"Right back," she said as she went to grab the drinks.

"Kaleem let's hit the VIP section."

"I'ma chill from that spot."

"Why?" Ta'Rod asked.

"Niggas be targets," he replied.

"These suckas' don't know us."

"You right, let's keep it that way."

"Fo'sho', I hear ya'."

When the DJ saw that Alicia Keys and Faith Evans were in the building, he shouted them some love. Stars would come and go all night. It was 3:00 a.m. and the club was still packed!

"I'm ready to bounce," Ta'Rod said.

"Word," Kaleem agreed.

They made their way towards the door, Kaleem felt a tug on his arm... it was Diaz. "Excuse me!" she said when he turned around, and continued, "You were going to just leave and not say nothing? You forgot the most important thing..." She slid her number in his hand.

"Guess I'm thinking too hard tonight, my bad sexy." He gave her a hug and another kiss on the cheek.

"I'm gonna put it on this motherfucker, he just doesn't know," she thought to herself.

"Later, baby girl,"

"Later, Mr. Brick City,"

In front of the club sits a white Bentley Maybach coupe that took the show. If ya' shit wasn't two hundred plus keep it moving, so they did!

"Back to the Brick City," he told Ta'Rod.

"You know it."

CHAPTER 4

Ten stacks. This was their biggest pick up yet. A half key, Santos will know they handle business.

Ta'Rod hit up Santos on the phone…

"Qué pasa?" Santos spoke as he answered his phone.

"I need a half a car. I have ten for you."

"Okay," he replied. "Is Kaleen with you?" he asked, pronouncing Kaleem's name wrong as always.

"Yeah, we together," Ta'Rod responded.

"This is what you need to do, this time, things have changed. Go to Willie Burgers on 145th and St. Nicholas; tell the señorita behind the counter that you called in an order for Brick City. Buy a box of washing powder, put the money inside, and reseal it. Then give it to the señorita behind the counter. Make sure your count is right! Got me?"

"Yeah,"

"Good, let me talk to Kaleen."

"Hello," Kaleem spoke into the phone.

"I will call you later, Ok." The phone went dead.

They did everything in order as they were told.

They parked on 140th Street and walked so the car wouldn't be noticable with the Jersey tags. Santos moved a lot of work and had the money to back it up. He never had to touch any work.

"I called in an order for Brick City," Ta'Rod told the Spanish chick behind the counter.

"See, Pope, I got you right here."

Kaleem passed her the money thinking, *"God has given the world some beautiful women. Damn, a text from Santos… How I miss that?"*

The text read,

"Loyalty is what distinguishes the professionals from the amateurs. Loyalty will secure you."

"He was right about that." Kaleem thought. *"It all goes back to the jokers that jump in the game, turn informant, snitch, and work for the Alphabet boys, they sell their soul.* He text back,

"Ain't no such thing as a halfway crook, they scared to death. That snitch shit is some bitch shit! I'ma body them all before they make me fall. I will be true. Loyalty is my bond."

* * *

7:00 a.m. Saturday morning it was a great day at Superior Barbershop, owned by Heavy 'D', a top of the line high-end shop; with four large front windows, four sixty-inch flat screens, a game room, and eight occupied booths with barbers cutting hair. Four of the barbers had side jobs while cutting hair. One sold coke, one weed, one pills, and the other heroin. Talk about a one-stop shop, the boosters came in and out, selling whatever all day. You can even place orders for what you want to wear that night.

"Peace, my black brothers," Bro Tariq said as he came in.

"As Salaam Alaikum, peace," Ta'Rod responded.

"My brothers, let me drop some wisdom on your souls. You see all the young black youths that are divided, hurt, confused, lost, or incarcerated. You see all the senseless killing going on around here. Don't you know the new Ku Klux Klan for the Twenty-first century wear black hoodies and faces are black?" Tariq told everyone sitting around in the barbershop, and continued, "We are our own worst enemy. We headed for self-destruction! We have the power to change. Allah can open those prison doors. We must realize the fight ain't against each other. The Devil knows he can't survive much longer. Many will ridicule you, but they did the same thing to Noah. They laughed at him!"

"I feel where you comin' from," one person said.

"Then what are you waiting for?" Bro Tariq asked.

"I'm not on that level." he responded.

"I hope it's not too late when you are."

"Please don't take my pork chops." Heavy 'D' said.

The whole shop laughed...

"I'm out of here; I just want you brothers to think." Bro Tariq stated, leaving something on their mind to think about.

* * *

Later that evening, Ta'Rod and Kaleem had made another trip to New York, now on their way headed back. They have been dealing with the connect for eight months now.

"Finish with the blunt so the car can air out before we hit the toll booth," Kaleem told Ta'Rod.

"This 'exotic' is some good shit!" Ta'Rod said toking on the blunt.

Jay-Z's *'I'm a hustler baby'* bumped through the car system speakers... *"And I want you to know It ain't where I been, but where I'm 'bout to go."*

Kaleem pulled up on the woman at the toll booth, "Hello, honey." she said passing him the ticket.

"Thanks. Have a nice day." Kaleem said and pulled off.

As they were driving, Kaleem spotted a motorcycle cop coming up fast behind them. The cop rolled up on the driver's side of the car, flashed his badge, and pointed for him to pull over.

"A fucking cop, what luck," Kaleem said in a frustrated tone.

"Don't panic. As long as the coke is sealed inside those crunch-n-munch boxes we good." Ta'Rod said.

Kaleem pulled over, put the car in park, and turned the car off. He thought to himself, *"A motorcycle cop ridin' an 1100 Suzuki... uh-uh."*

The cop walked up to the driver's window. "Good afternoon, fellas. License and registration," he stated to Kaleem while looking around in the car.

"Yes, Sir, may I ask why you pulled me over?"

He didn't answer, just walked back to his bike.

The man was big. He was about two-hundred and fifty solid, dressed in all black leather, and had mirrored shades on.

"Kaleem watched him through the rear-view. He took a backpack off the bike and started walking back toward the car.

Ta'Rod and Kaleem sat there trying to figure out what he was doing, something just didn't seem right.

"Kaleem," he said as he approached the window. "Mr. Santos sent you this package. He will be in touch," he stated, walked back to his bike, hopped on, and rode off...

"If Santos is connected like that so are we, Ta'Rod."

"We in the game now," Ta'Rod responded.

"You know this ain't no game and I know that he has already seen who is who in Newark already. So I know we got to play fair!"

"Absolutely," Ta'Rod agreed.

CHAPTER 5

Back in Newark on Howard Street, everybody was on the porch and sidewalk hanging out. As Kaleem and Ta'Rod pulled up, Kayson rolled through in his gray coupe V-12 Benz– It was only two in the hood. Kayson was the only kid in high school that had a brand new Jaguar. Everyone knew he was a businessperson. Word was he had a few houses out of town.

"What's good?" they both spoke, as they greeted the people going inside the building.

While they were waiting for the elevator, Kaleem put his gun in his hand, hiding it on the side of his leg just in case somebody tried something stupid. You had to be on point, even in the elevator you had to make sure nobody was riding in the shaft. *Can't get caught slippin.*

Knock, Knock,

"Who is it?" a voice answered.

"Kaleem and Ta'Rod," Kaleem responded.

"Hey, baby," Pat greeted as she let them inside. "You smell good, Kaleem, what you have on?"

"She got to have it."

"Ha, ha, ha, your crazy ass. Hey, Ta'Rod,"

"Hi, Pat. Ain't nothing, just chillin',"

"You here by yourself?" Kaleem asked.

"Yeah, why?" she answered.

"We just got back from the city and I need to separate a few things."

"Do what you do. The kids are gone."

"Pass me the backpack, Ta'Rod."

"Damn a whole brick!" Kaleem said anxiously.

"That's what I'm talkin' 'bout," Ta'Rod replied.

"Who y'all rob?" Pat asked curiously.

"You know we don't roll like that," Kaleem answered. "This some fire, we need to put some cut on this."

"The best cut to use is procaine. It's expensive, but it is worth every dollar." Ta'Rod said.

"Pat here is a hundred. Go downtown to Spain's Restaurant and grab us some seafood. Unless you gone fry some fish today; you know I love ya' fish,"

"Well, you damn sure won't love me today, because ya' girlfriend is off. I got you, though," she said jokingly.

"Don't forget to call me when you do Pat."

"I got you," she stated.

"Nothing can happen to this coke." Kaleem thought.

"Oh, yeah, I forgot to tell y'all," as Pat went on, "I'm glad y'all didn't come 'bout two hours earlier."

"Why?" Kaleem asked.

"Because some guys came on the block from Elizabeth Avenue looking for Haas,"

"What!" they exclaimed.

"Yeah, he robbed them last night. They came from West Kenny Street side building 218. The crazy thing is they didn't realize they were talking to Haas. They didn't know it was Haas, so they asked him where was Haas at, and that they were his cousins. Haas said yeah, he lives on the fourth-floor apartment 4B."

"I thought that apartment was abandoned," Kaleem said.

"You're right, it is," Pat replied, and went on. "Let me finish telling you. Three guys got on the elevator and rode up to the fourth floor. So, Hass ran up the stairs. They started knocking on the door, and Haas came from out the stairway shooting... one bullet hit one dude in the back, and the other in his arm, only to spend him around to catch the bullet Haas put into his forehead. The last guy got it in his chest, but he is still alive."

"Damn," Ta'Rod said.

"Haas is a beast when it comes to putting in work," Ta'Rod stated.

"You ain't lying about that," Pat agreed.

"His hands are as deadly as his guns," Kaleem said.

The streets knew Haas played no games. They will be glad when he retires!

CHAPTER 6

Three weeks after Ta'Rod and Kaleem had the brick of coke, everyone was wanting it! It was good work and they all knew it.

This Saturday at the Barbershop, it was full as always. Some of the fattest rides were parked out front. Springfield Avenue kept a lot of traffic… a car and truck show all day. People came from New York, Philly, Delaware, PA, and Maryland.

"Heavy 'D', less talking and more cutting," Kaleem stated.

"I am cutting." he replied.

"Am I next?" Kaleem asked impatiently, ready to get out of there.

"Yeah, come on,"

Once in the barber chair, Heavy 'D' put a towel over his mouth, "Hold this right here!"

"Ha, ha, you got jokes right?"

Anytime Kaleem sat in the barber chair, he automatically put his Glock .40 on his lap, keeping it pointed at the door with his finger on the trigger. *Never let your guards down.*

"Hey, Kaleem,"

"What's up, George? When you bringin' that broke ass jump shot to the court again?"

George was called, Lil Jordan. His game was nice! "I'm comin' out Sunday joker."

"You can find ya' man at a barber shop,"

"What's good Rajohn?"

"Chillin',"

"That's what it is, you still got my number, hit me if you need me."

"That's what it is, fo' sho'," Rajohn replied.

"What's up, Nito?" Kaleem greeted as he came through the door with a pretty white girl; blonde hair, blue eyes, hair past her shoulders, and stacked at about one hundred and twenty-five pounds, "Nito that's your girl?"

"This my Barbie doll," he said with a smile.

"Where she from?"

"South Jersey, Asbury Park,"

"What's her name?"

"Damn, Kaleem, ask her she can talk!"

"Well, what's your name, Ms. South Jersey?"

"Michelle," she responded.

"How do you like the hood? Nothin' like home, is it?"

"I can handle it. It has its diversities,"

"I'ma come down and find me a Barbie,"

"Tell Nito to bring you, I got friends."

Kaleem looked over at Nito sitting in the chair and said, "You hear that?"

"Excuse me," a woman said as she walked in the Barbershop, "do you have a restroom I can use?"

"Right by the games," Heavy D' told her.

She was thick, brown skinned complexion and attractive; carrying a big brown shoulder bag. She had on a big white tee, white on white air forces and blue jeans. No one paid much attention because she went right in the bathroom.

Five minutes later, "Damn!" someone said.

"What the fuck!" Ta'Rod replied.

"Look!" someone yelled as she bent over and touched the floor with both hands, naked…

"Welcome to the hood," Kaleem said to the Barbie. "The show must go on!"

Nito's white friend was amazed. Heavy 'D' had finished Nito's cut and he had to leave. Somebody put the close sign on the door fast.

"Let the show begin," one man said.

This woman was surely a dancer; she knew how to get the crowded shop of men aroused! "I'm about my money. I charge one fifty for the works, no anal, and no taken pictures of my face. If you ain't got no condom, ain't nothin' goin' in me," she stated with authority.

Mack is a high roller, he ran next door and bought ten boxes of magnum condoms and grabbed his camera out the trunk of his Lexus.

"I'm first," Heavy 'D' said.

"I take two at a time daddy!"

"Damn," one man said.

"Just call me, Honey," she said. "I am goin' to lie on the floor, and I want someone to lite these candles and let them drip all over my body while I am rubbin' my pussy."

"Oh yes, ooh yes! This is what I'm talkin' 'bout," Rajohn said.

"The wax makes me cum, cum, and cum. Yes, burn me, baby!"

Everyone's manhood was standing at attention, being turned on by the show she was producing. She stopped moving to allow the wax to drip all over her body. Then she was ready to reach her climax and erupt like a volcano. Her body shattered the wax into little pieces. She counted her cash, bent over and continued. Heavy D' stuck his erect manhood inside of her from the back, while she sucked off Fireman Fu's hose between his legs. Honey had no problem taking Fireman Fu testicles inside her mouth as she sucked his penis. She made both men cum at the same time.

Next up was Ta'Rod and Rajohn. Honey rode Ta'Rod as if she was in a rodeo, bouncing up and down. The sounds that came from the juices of her body turned all of them on. Rajohn was so cool he just laid back like a boss and let Honey allow him to explode in her mouth.

The final show that she gave them took the cake. She took a long neck Budweiser bottle, turned it upside down and with no hands, she squatted down on top of it nice and smooth until the bottle disappeared. When she stood up and bent over, no one could see the bottle! She was good at what she did. Bobby wanted to keep her longer, but Heavy 'D' had to open the shop back up. She passed out business cards after she got dressed before she left.

CHAPTER 7

"Ta'Rod, take a ride with me across town," Kaleem asked.

"Why? What's up?"

"I wanna check out this cutie I met downtown last week,"

"She got any friends?" Ta'Rod inquired.

"I told you I just met her,"

"I can't stay over there long,"

"I hope you not tryin' to cut now?"

"I'll go with ya', hold on let me holla' at Kaleef.... Yo' Kaleef,"

"What's good Ta'Rod? I will be back in a few. I'ma need you to bring me my girlfriend right fast." Ta'Rod stated.

"Okay, one minute."

"Girlfriend," Kaleem said.

"Relax! My girlfriend is my gun; when I need her to bust, she busts.

"Here you go, Ta'Rod," Kaleef said as he passed him the gun.

"Hold shit down until I get back, Kaleef."

"I got you."

* * *

Kaleem and Ta'Rod pulled up to Kim's townhouse on Thirteenth Street and Sixteenth Avenue. Many people were outside hanging around. From the looks of it, you could see money comes on the block. When Kim saw Kaleem, she walked over to the car. She was wearing a pink and white Baby Phat sweat suit, brown skinned, dreads, and a Halley Berry figure.

"What's good, sweetheart?" Kaleem said as she reached the car.

"How are you, Mr.? I didn't think you were coming."

"It's not like that. This is my partner, Ta'Rod,"

"What's up, Kim?" Ta'Rod spoke.

"Hey, how you doin?"

"Yeah, I came to see what you were talkin' about the block getting money."

"Yeah, these guys around here don't know how to treat the people that be putting food on their table or money in their pocket."

"Word," Ta'Rod said.

"So you sayin' you can handle getting money?" Kaleem stated.

"Don't let the looks fool ya'. See I'ma gangsta', bitch! I get down for my crown. I ain't slow," she stated with attitude.

"You get high?" Kaleem asked.

"Never have, gotta stay on point. Like I told you, I ain't got time for no games; I got two kids that must be straight."

"I am feelin' you, Kim, I will see what you can do, just follow the game plan and you can cake."

"When you talkin' 'bout? I have to get a few of my girls on point."

"I'ma call you," Kaleem said.

"Kim, you got someone I can meet?" Ta'Rod asked.

"My girl, Endy, she is a baby doll."

"Give her my number…" Ta'Rod gave her the number and she stored it in her phone.

"You got a gun, Kim?" Kaleem wanted to know.

"I'm good with them; I told you I'm a gangsta!" she said.

"So you think I can come by tonight and cut?"

"You know how shit goes, Kaleem, I can't be getting hooked on your ass if I'ma be focused on getting this money. A bitch got plans."

"That's what it is. I guess we can do it before you start working," he responded. They both laughed.

* * *

Getting paid in full…

Thirteenth, North Seventh, Court, Central Avenue, Avon Avenue, Irvin Tuner Boulevard, Little Bricks, West End Avenue, Bergan Avenue, Twenty-first Street, and Twenty-Second Street in Irvington New Jersey. Everyone wanted that good coke at a good price. Shit was jumping! Kaleem and Ta'Rod had bought a money counter for two hundred, but it broke down. So they got another for two stacks.

Kaleem's conscience stays on his mind, telling him shit like, *"They are going to kill you! Stop while you can!"* Not a day go by that he wake up and don't think it could be his last day alive. The money was coming so fast, it was crazy. He had miss counted twenty thousand dollars and didn't realize it until he looked in a brown bag three weeks later, and there it was! So much stuff was going on at one time. It wasn't like the old days, 'Brick City' downtown Newark, like being at the Adams Movie Theater on Bradford Place checking out Bruce Lee Karate flicks, or the Paramount on Market Street, jewelry stores, clothing, sneakers, and anything else you needed; Vendors on every corner, the YMCA and Library. Penny Arcade, Twin City Skating, music, girls, guys, and catching the twenty-four buses there. Dayton Street projects rolled deep, looking to catch a person slipping, if they did, just empty your pockets or take the beat down, and then they will empty them. Penn Station will get you anywhere, outstanding Spanish restaurants, Spain's, Iberia, and Don 21. What if things never changed? What if?

Kim wasn't joking. In just three weeks, she was moving nine ounces a week in twenties. She wrapped her coke inside of aluminum foil. That's how people knew it was hers.

Kaleem took a ride over to Kim's spot... It was only eight at night and the spot was jumping. As she said, she had girls on her team. A few guys were running up to cars, that was crazy. Doing some shit like that, you'll be liable to get your face blown off.

A black Beemer pulled up with tinted windows, sat there for ten minutes, and nobody got out.

"This shit don't look right." Kaleem thought to himself. He grabbed his phone to call Kim, no answer... *"Why the hell she ain't got no lookout!"* he thought. He tried calling her again...

"Yeah, this Kim, leave a message..."

"Damn!"

"Hey, Jerry, you saw that black BMW parked down the block?" Kim said to her girl on the phone.

"Yeah, with three guys getting out, that's stick up."

"Just give them the shit when they get to ya',"

"Don't panic I can make it to the door," Jerry responded.

"No, do what I say," Kim replied.

"Lara and I are on top of shit, okay, Kim?"

The three stickup men went right to the porch to Jerry and searched her. They took some cash and coke. Two people had stopped by the Beemer, but they kept walking to the corner.

"She told me she had guns and nobody strapped." Kaleem thought.

Three guys ran and jumped in their car and pulled off. The two tires on the right side were both flat with sparks flying from the rims. The car made it to the corner, and then two people in hoodies started shooting inside the Beemer...

Baca! Baca! Baca!

Tac! Tac! Tac!

Baca, Bac!

"Let me get the fuck outta here fast!" Kaleem said to himself. His tires peeled as he hauled ass before the popo came.

* * *

Nine o'clock the next morning, Kaleem phone went off, it was a text from Kim saying: **Sorry I didn't get back to you last night, hit me up!**

Instead of returning the text, he called her back...

"Hello," Kim answered.

"Damn, the phone didn't even ring yet!" Kaleem said.

"I was about to call somebody," Kim responded.

"What's the deal?" he asked.

"Everything good, some lame ass jokers tried us last night! They took too long, that put me on point."

"You know who it was?" Kaleem asked.

"Nah, but check what happen, they know about this block, though. My girl Jerry had the work on her, which was nothing big, and a few hundred, I told her to give it to them when they came to her, while me and my girl, Lara went out the back door of the apartment and stab two of the tires on their car. When they got close to the corner of the block, me and Lara dumped on 'em; dumped almost two clips into the car. The crazy thing they all lived. But I promise they got the message loud and clear!"

"I see you are the gangsta' bitch like you said, huh?"

"Some guys think girls don't bust guns!" she said. "Anyway, that small shit is over now. The block is good, that's why I wanted them to be driving off. I got seven stacks for you. After the next re-up, I will be buying my own work from you."

"That's what's up."

Kim was on point. Her next pick-up she gave him twelve five for a half brick, *she was working.*

CHAPTER 8

Kaleem picked Queen up from the hospital, to take her on a lunch date.

"Damn she seemed to make the sun hotter, with the rays from her booty. I mean beauty! She is surely a showstopper!" Kaleem thought to himself. "Hi, Queen, how are you feeling today?" he asked.

"Good,"

"Good is not a feelin'," he said.

"Well, Kaleem, I feel blessed."

"Now, that you are. Were you busy today at work?"

"No, not really. Where are we having lunch? I know a nice park in Morristown, New Jersey off Speedwell Avenue. It's a real nice park, you will like it," she told him.

They rode up Interstate Highway 280 listening to Tupac…

"So you enjoy Pac music also?" Kaleem asked.

"Yes. I admire all his positive songs."

"His lyrics spit a lot of wisdom,"

"I agree," she stated.

"I got everything ready for our outing, she will know that I'm Mr. Lover Man and I'm not talkin' Shaba Ranks." Kaleem thought to himself.

"This is my first time riding in a Corvette. You have a nice car, Kaleem,"

"Thank you, but it's not mine, it's my friend, Wali's."

"He has got to be a good friend to let you use it,"

"Once I told him about you, he told me to come get it. I think the color gold is why I really like it, it's my favorite color."

Once they got to the park, Kaleem grabbed the Nike bag that had everything inside, laid out the big blanket, and started laying out everything else. They had two garden salads, townhouse crackers, cheese, Chardonnay White wine, and a portable CD player with the sounds of 'Sade' in the air.

"Kaleem, so where do you see yourself in the next five years?"

"Damn that was a head shot." Kaleem thought.

The question blew him away and the truth scared the hell out of him. He knew she did not want to hear jail or hell. And those two things wouldn't open her doors at all.

"I want a wife and kids. I also want to help my city," he finally answered.

"What type of work you do again?"

"I'm an auto technician." he quickly lied.

"So you fix cars!"

"Yeah," he answered and they began to laugh.

"The beauty that she passed, was so radiant, she shined from her glowing green eyes to her golden brown hair. She had class and style. The body she was blessed with will make women and men want her.

"I am overwhelmed by your personality. The beauty that comes from your inside over-rides your appearance."

"I appreciate that. Thank you," she replied.

"I call it the way it is, baby,"

"I can still hear your mom's speaking on how much she love you and don't want the streets to take you away from her. Now we both know the streets have robbed many of the young black men in our society every day," she continued. "I mean in our hoods we have Lawyers, Doctors, Business Owners, Presidents, and Scientist."

"I know what you are saying. It is a jungle out there, you never know what to expect from the streets— and ain't nothin' comin' for free, not at all." Kaleem said.

"As you see, I don't deal with a lot of people. I have a lot going on with work and church," she said.

Kaleem couldn't seem to figure out the feeling he had when he was around her. But one thing he did know was that she wasn't his. That made it one hell of a challenge. The beauty that God provides to this earth is so beautiful, especially when you can experience it with someone you love.

They sat, talked, ate, and watched the nice sight of the swans gliding across the pond with the trees in full bloom.

"I hope you enjoyed our lunch," he told her.

"It was lovely. Thank you, Kaleem."

After packing everything up, they headed back to the car. He opened the door for her to get in, and then closed it when she was completely inside. As he got in the driver's seat and started the car, 'Whip Appeal' by Baby Face thumped through the Boss system.

"Kaleem, I would like for you to meet someone."

"Who is that?"

"My mother, Inez; she lives in Jersey City on Claremont Avenue."

"Sure, I would love to meet her,"

"When?" she asked.

"We can go now if you have the time."

"Alright, cool, let's start heading that way." he stated.

As they were riding, Kaleem thought about some guys over there still on that young boy shit that doesn't like them from Newark. Although he knew a few Heavy Hitters over there like Roc, Kemo, Quzzie-Qua, Man and Big Jay, he still had to make sure he was on point.

When Kaleem pulled up on Ocean Avenue and Claremont in front of Neil's Liquor Store, it was a crowd of people outside checking Wali's Corvette out as he parked.

"Do you know a lot of people around here?" he asked.

"My mom's been around here for fifteen years."

"Just checkin', I never liked big crowds," he responded.

As soon as Queen got out and closed the car door, Kaleem placed his nine millimeter in his pants pocket, got out the car and then set the car alarm.

"What's up? What's up?" some people in the crowd said.

"What's up wit' cha'?" Kaleem spoke, and they kept it moving making their way into the apartment building.

When they made it to the second floor, she knocked on the door…

"Who is it?" a soft voice asked.

"It's your daughter, Ma!"

When the door opened, Kaleem saw the eyes of an Indian looking woman with lovely gray and black hair.

"Hello, honey," she said.

"Hi, Ma, this is, Kaleem." Queen said, and then went on to say, "Kaleem, this is my mom's, Inez."

"Hello, how are you?" he replied and asked.

"Fine, I'm blessed. How are you?"

"Great. Thank you."

"Nice to meet you, Kaleem,"

"Ok," he replied.

"Ma, let's see what is in the kitchen."

"Okay, come on."

While they were in the kitchen, Kaleem's phone started going off vibrating. "Yo', what's the deal homie?" Ta'Rod said when he answered.

"Ain't shit over in JC,"

"What the hell you over there for?"

"Handlin' a few things," he told him, not wanting to expose his hand with Queen yet.

"Well, when you finish bullshittin' swing by the spot,"

"That's what it is," he replied and ended the call just in time as they re-entered the living room.

"Kaleem, son, do you believe in God?" Inez asked.

"Ma!" Queen yelled.

"Nah, its ok, allow me to answer her," Kaleem stated and then said, "Yes I do Ms. Inez. I am a young black man that always had to fight and prove myself to get things in life. They say that America is the land of the free, that's some BS, excuse my French. Look at all the brave men and women that fought wars for our freedom just to be double-crossed by the same ones that run America. I want the same dreams the next man wants."

"You seem to be an intelligent young man," Inez continued, "but I hear a lot of anger and pain as well. I want you to read something, give me a minute please."

"Sure," he replied.

"My mother loves God as you can tell."

"Here it is I'll read it. It's called the pencil; The pencil maker took the pencil aside. Just before putting it into the box and said, 'There are five things you need to know before I send you out into the world. Always remember them and you will become the best pencil in the world. One, you will be able to do great things, only if you allow yourself to be held in someone's hand. Two, you will experience some painful sharpening from time to time, but you will become better. Three, you will be able to correct mistakes that you will make. Four, the most important part of you will be what's on the inside. Five, on every surface you are used, you must leave your mark no matter of the condition you must continue to write. Have a purpose replace the pencil with yourself. The author of that is unknown, so let us just say it is one of God's Angles!"

"Thank, you Ms. Inez for the wisdom you shared with me. I'm sorry, but I have to get back to Newark to take care of some business."

"No problem, now that you know where I live, feel free to come visit me."

"I sure will." he said and gave her a hug before leaving.

"Make sure you drive safe with my daughter."

"Not a problem," he replied.

"Okay, Ma, I love you and will call you later."

"Okay, Queen, love you too, baby."

As soon as they walked out the building, Kaleem saw a guy sitting on the Vette. He chirped the alarm, and the guy got off.

"My bad." the guy said.

Kaleem nodded, hoping not to have to use the nine in his pocket. They hopped in the car and drove off.

Queen took a quick nap, as the ride ended they were back at the hospital on Bergen Street. He got out and opened her door to let her out, "Thank you for such a good time today." she said.

They embraced each other with a hug, with him not wanting to let her go. He finally released the bear hug he was giving her. *"Damn that felt good,"* he thought to himself. He watched her gorgeous self-disappear inside the hospital.

CHAPTER 9

It has been a week now since Kaleem saw Ms. Inez. For some reason, he couldn't get this lady out of his mind. He had Semen's Furniture store refurbish an old grandfather clock of his so that he could give it as a gift to Ms. Inez. He had been a long time customer of theirs, so they hooked him up with a good price. He had them build a stash box inside of it, and he put fifty thousand dollars and a .40-Glock in it. *One day she will be blessed with the cash and protection.*

Kaleem picked up his phone and called Ms. Inez. "Hello," a soft voice answered.

"Hello, Ms. Inez, this is Kaleem, your daughter friend."

"Yes, how are you, sweetie?"

"I'm good. I had you on my mind and brought you a gift. Is it okay if I bring it to you? I hope you don't mind."

"Of course not," she continued, "do you realize many people never sit down and try to understand their purpose or motives in life? They can't see God is always by their side. My daughter is a sweet girl. Her job keeps her busy. That was a surprise to see her with you."

"I agree she is a nice girl."

"You must remember son, whatever God does is for the best."

"Okay, I got it. Ms. Inez, I'm bringing the gift today."

"Alright, I'll be home."

"Okay, goodbye." they said their goodbyes and disconnected the call.

* * *

Kaleem was en route following behind the delivery truck to Ms. Inez place to drop off her gift. He gave her a call letting her know to be expecting him because he will be pulling up in a minute.

After they pulled up and parked, the movers unloaded the grandfather clocked wrapped in a thick blanket and hauled it up to Ms. Inez.

"Hello, Kaleem," Ms. Inez said as she met him at the door.

"Hi, this is the gift I got for you; I hope you like it," he said, as the movers unveiled the clock.

"It is beautiful," she said with a smile. "This is so nice of you, what a blessing for me. Thank you, Kaleem."

"You're welcome. I'm glad I was able to give it."

The movers took the grandfather clock inside her house and placed it where she wanted it, right in her living room against the wall in a corner.

"Don't forget son," she went on to say, "whatever God does, is for the best, and once again, I am very thankful."

"Yes Ma'am," he responded.

"You take care of yourself," she told him and gave him a hug.

"I will." He and the mover left out with her locking the door behind them…

Kaleem turned to the movers, "I appreciate you two bringing it over here for me here is an extra fifty."

"Thanks, anytime, Kaleem." the head mover said.

* * *

While riding back over to Brick City, Kaleem kept replaying in his head what Ms. Inez was saying, *"Whatever God does is for the best..."*

He pushed through traffic in deep thought about his life...

"What's up Kaleem? I'm Mr. Devil, you know me?" a voice spoke. The Devil stayed in Kaleem's head, up to no good... *"You don't have time to be chasing no ass! You need to get this fast money. Don't worry about your family, long as you give them shit, they don't care what you do. The streets will have all your time anyway! You don't have time to be a father, son, brother or uncle. Don't worry about going to jail, pay up when they catch up. The only thing you will have to pay is a Bails Bondman, a Lawyer, fines, and canteen. I'm on your side I will never leave you. I'm out of your head for now, but I promise I'll be back, Kaleem!"*

"Fuck what you sayin'," he thought. Kaleem tried to shake the Devil thoughts out his head. He picked up his phone and dialed Queen's number...

Ring... Ring...

"Hello, how are you, Queen?" Kaleem began as she answered the line.

"I'm blessed. How are you, Kaleem?" she responded and continued. "For a minute I didn't think you saw the number." Assuming he would have called sooner.

"I didn't want to push you. By the way, it's a show coming up soon and I would love for you to be my guest."

"What show?" she asked.

"Frankie Beverly and Maze, Toni Braxton, and Howard Hewitt, I think?"

"I enjoy all of their music. When is it? "She asked in excitement.

"It's September seventh, a Saturday night."

"I will make sure I'm not on call that day."

"You know you're my soul-mate, Queen?"

"How can you know that and don't truly know me?" thinking he could be just running game on her; she would soon find out...

"You are heaven-sent by God," he told her.

"You certainly have a way with words, don't you sir?"

"Sometimes," he said with confidence. "By the way, how is your mom?"

"She is good. She really likes her clock. You didn't have to do that."

"It was an old clock I had fixed up. I thought it would make a good gift. After all the spiritual insight she gives me, that's priceless."

"Well, that was nice of you to do that."

Changing the subject, "Maybe I can have you... I mean, take you to dinner." Kaleem slid in.

"We will have to see about that," Queen stated playing hard to get. "Well, Mr. I'm about to go to sleep."

"I will be happy to come assist you with that," Kaleem said, hoping she would bite.

"How many women have you said that to this month?"

"I was waiting to tell you."

"Yeah, right," she replied not believing him. "I'm sorry I must decline your offer tonight."

"If you change your mind, feel free to hit me up. Have a blessed night."

"Good night, Kaleem."

"Good night. One more thing..." he said before hanging up, "I want you Queen, and I'm going to wait for you." *Was he moving too fast?* To him, it didn't hurt to try.

"Good night, Kaleem." she said as a smile crossed her face, and then she hung up the phone.

* * *

Queen laid in her King size bed with her red Victoria Secret sexy pajama set on. She laid there thinking about how she felt an attraction to Kaleem. She couldn't get him off her mind. *She was playing hard to get.*

Knock, Knock, Knock,

"Who is it?" Queen asked.

"It's Kaleem,"

"Hi, Kaleem, what are you doing here?"

"Queen, I want to explore every single inch of your body tonight."

Kaleem grabbed Queen by her hand and walked her to her bedroom. As he walked through her house, he admired her lovely decorated house; the furniture was nice solid oak, and the smell of flowers and oils filled the room. When they entered her room, Queen walked over to her CD player and turned it on— BabyFace *'Ready or Not'* flowed through the speakers. Kaleem sang to the words of the song as he slowly laid her across the bed, "I'll give you everything and more, all that I got– is yours..." slowly undressing one another.

As he sang along Queen's emotions had taken over her at that point. He caressed her body with his strong, soft hands. *"Ooh, I know I'm tight, not been touched in fifteen years."* she thought with a smirk on her face.

He kissed her sensually from her plumped lips to her now hardened nipples. He massaged her wet kitty with his hardwood. "Aah," she let out a soft moan. He entered in her slow, playing with the cat– inserting his meaty head in and out...

"Ooh, yeah!" she yelled out in ecstasy as he pushed it in deep and hard...

"Daddy, daddy, don't stop... please, yeah, right there."

"Yeah, take this dick," he said as he pounded her juice box.

"Yes, mmm, mmm," she moaned out in pleasure as she began to cream all over his shiny pole.

"Damn, this dick is good." Queen thought to herself smiling, biting her bottom lip.

The sounds of the smacking of Kaleem going in and out of her had her coming back to back.

She flipped him over on his back, putting his meaty manhood in his mouth; giving him the pleasure that every man desired. She had his dick very wet– kissing, licking, and sucking it vigorously. She had him standing at attention, rock solid; eyes closed, toes curled. Her head was in complete motion– up and down, round and round...

"Cum for me, daddy," she told him as she sucked on him continuously, stroking him with a hand.

"Aww, ooh, yeah, baby," he said as he let out warm thick white semen in her mouth. *She swallowed it all...*

Queen puts his testicles in her mouth and he stood right up and came back to life. She sat on him inserting his hardwood deep inside her wet box and worked him; she rode him like a stallion.

"Fuck me, Queen. Give it to me, baby!" he yelled as he exploded inside of her.

He flipped her over, spread her legs, and tasted her sweet juices; slurping it all up. He massaged his head as he licked and sucked on her hardened clitoris.

"This is the best sex I have ever had...," she said to herself.

The sound of Queen's phone woke her up out her sleep...

"No I didn't!" she yelled as she jumped up, missing the phone call.

The bed was wet all over; her panties and pajamas were soaked. She had had a wet dream about Kaleem. She had been having wet dreams for a little over a week now. The effect he had on her was crazy because they had never even kissed before. *What was this?*

* * *

Queen picked up her phone and called Cookie. "Hey, girl," she spoke when Cookie picked up.

"Hey, what's up, girl?"

Queen went on to say, "Do you remember that nice guy, Kaleem? The one I told you I had lunch with in the park.

My mom is feeling him too. He gave her a nice grandfather clock a few weeks back."

"Bitch will you get to the point!" Cookie demanded.

"Well, I've been having wet dreams about him for over a week now."

"Shit, you haven't had sex in fifteen years what you expect! Girl, it couldn't be me,"

"I think I love him. That's the crazy thing."

"So what are you going to do?" Cookie asked.

"There is nothing I can do."

"I know I'm sorry for asking that. We have been girls ever since six grade, I'ma always be with you and pray with you, Queen. God will work out everything he always does. Plus, I don't want you to drown in all that stuff coming out of you!" they both laughed.

"Well, I'll talk to you later. I needed to get that off my chest. I love you."

"I love you too." they both hung up.

"I need to pull myself together. I am really falling for this guy. I can't let him know, though. I got too much stuff going on with me." Queen thought to herself.

CHAPTER 10

"The surgery went very well the other day," Dr. Hopkins told Kaleem.

"Can I see her now?" Kaleem asked.

"Sure. She will be released today as well."

"I can't thank you and your staff enough, doctor."

"Not a problem, at all. Take care and have a good day."

"You do the same."

"Hi, Ma," Kaleem spoke as he entered his mother's room, greeting her with a hug and a kiss.

"Hi, baby, how are you?"

"I'm good, ma. You know the doctor said you can leave today?"

"Yes, he told me, son."

"Also, Aunt Gert wants you to come down to Virginia. She set everything up for you. I thought that the move would do you good."

"What about my apartment?" she asked concerned.

"Taken care of already; I packed all your things up and put it in storage."

"What about my security deposit?"

"I took care of that. If you agree, you will leave in three days. The family will have a chance to see you before you go. Ja'Mia and Trehzer will drive you down."

"How are they doing?"

"They doing good, still getting good grades going to Howard University."

"What about you, Kaleem?"

"I'll be fine, Ma. Plus, I will be coming to visit you. My main concern is you. You know I'm Brick City…

"I know son for Life," she told him as she interrupted what he was saying.

"You got it Ma, Brick City 4 Life," he continued saying.

"I will keep praying for you, son. Be safe, Kaleem."

"I will, Ma."

"You sure you packed all my things?"

"I had a party and a lot got broken," he said.

"I know you done bumped your head now," she said.

"Yeah, Ma, I packed everything."

"You think you're my father sometimes don't you?"

"Kind of, nah I just love my mother. You ready to bounce out this place?"

"Yes, I'm ready. I want to leave a thank you card and some flowers."

"I paid for a large arrangement of flowers going to the nurse's station for you."

"So you do know your mother, huh? Thank you, honey, I love you, sweetie."

"I love you to Ma, we all we got!" Kaleem stated.

"Ms. Mack treated me real good while I was here."

"Yes, she is a blessing." he agreed.

CHAPTER 11

As Kaleem was on his way to the park, he thought, *"The big game is today. Let me see what's up with Queen."*

"Hello," Queen said as she answered her phone.

"What's good, Queen? I got a basketball game at Branch Brook Park and wanted to know if you wanted to check it out tonight at seven?"

"My girlfriend and I will be at the mall then."

"Make sure you buy me something," Kaleem jokingly stated.

"You seem to have what you need."

"I don't have you, Queen."

"You're making me blush. I hope you have a good game."

"Ok, give me a call later."

"Ok, Kaleem, goodbye."

By the time he hung up, he was already pulling up to pick up Ta'Rod. "Yo', what's the deal Ta'Rod?" he greeted as Ta'Rod came to the car.

"Ain't shit. Damn, you look lost Kaleem! Man, that hoe at the hospital got you fucked up!

"That's one thing, she ain't no hoe," Kaleem answered.

"Easy, it's just a figure of speech. You get that ass yet?"

"Nah, she ain't breakin'."

"You give up any cash?"

"She don't care about that either."

"Come on man get ya' head right, we got to turn shit up at that park tonight. They are expectin' 'Surprise' to win! The park will be off the hook," Ta'Rod said.

"We got our whole team so it's going down," Kaleem said, pulling up to the park. "It's already packed and it's just six o'clock. It ain't nowhere to park!"

"Just hit the security guard off in the Collenades," Ta'Rod said. The guard had no problem making the quick twenty.

Before every game, Ta'Rod sat on the bench and listened to D-Block and Styles P to get in his zone; he loved his music. The honeys were deep, all over the park. Cars doubled parked up and down Norfolk Street. Seventh Avenue was packed as well.

"How are you, Lil Dave?" Kaleem asked.

"Ready to show my ass, it's packed out in this bitch," he said, and then asked, "where Ta'Rod and Na'eem?"

"You know Ta'Rod on his music."

"There go Big Wali and Na'eem!" yelled Lil Dave.

"What's up Nyfice?" Kaleem spoke.

"Na'eem, how are you?" Lil Dave asked.

"Chillin', chillin'," Na'eem responded.

"Damn. Look at them two chicks with the Lakers Jersey dresses on." Kaleem said pointing in their direction. Their dresses were cut in a slant on one side with fishnet coming up the side and diamonds around the numbers.

Blacktop at night, they get it in with DJ Qua and Baseem on the mic and wheels of steel. Brick City, it's how they got down! 'Showtime' had beat 'Fat Joe's Terror Squad by two points last weekend at Rutgers Park in New

York. Therefore, 'Showtime' players were feeling themselves.

"Na'eem, is security in place before we get dress?" Kaleem inquired.

"Let me see, because I ain't seen Moose yet!"

"Yo,' what's gravy?" asked Moose as he answered his cell.

"Are your people in place, Moose?"

"You already know, Na'eem, I'm on it. I'm lookin' at you right now. Tell Kaleem, I saw him undressin' them two girls in the Lakers outfits, he looked like a stalker," they both laughed.

Na'eem knew Moose was on it. "Y'all wearin' the white jerseys tonight?" asked Moose.

"Right,"

"That's the business I got y'all. I got heat all up in here if it gets out of hand."

With all the betting on the sideline, sometimes assholes would try to play with your cash. The police station was right around the corner on Summer Avenue. Everyone knew this game would be hot. Two camera operators were on the scene taken pictures of the big event.

Momeen Dickey rolled up in a titanium color Rolls Royce Phantom V-12 that sat on twenty-four-inch Asanti chrome rims. Momeen had moved and wasn't able to come check out his people as often. However, he was well loved by his city.

"Big, Wali ain't that..."

"Hey, Wali, you ain't shit," Kesha said, going off.

"I was just goin' to call you last night," Big Wali told her.

"Yo' ass had me waitin' all night! Then pull a 'No Show'. Who in the hell you think you are, Mr. Only Dick around, I don't think so!" Kesha walked off, throwing her ass from side to side making sure the men eyes followed.

"I see she put yo' ass in check, Big Wali," Kaleem said laughing.

"My Mr. Only Dick, she loves, though." he replied.

"Hold on, let me speak to someone right fast," Kaleem said. "Saleemah, how are you sexy?"

"Hey, Kaleem, you playing today?"

"Yeah, I'ma do a little something."

"Good luck. Take this hug with you," she told him, reaching out for a hug.

"Woman you're still soft as ever."

"I gotta keep my skin pretty and soft," she said with confidence.

"I will get at you, it's 'bout game time," Kaleem said.

"Okay, talk to you later, Kaleem."

"Everybody to the bench!" Coach Jarell yelled. "Fellas just to let you know, it's a few people say we can beat 'Surprise'. Kayson just bet Doc twenty grand on us! We the real And-1; we got so much NBA material. Some never escapes the ghetto, but you all have a promising future on or off the court. So go hard! "Na'eem make sure you help handle the ball. I want them to run all over the court tonight. Keep pumpin' the ball down low to Wali and Ta'Rod. If that ain't happen kick the ball back out for the jump shots. I want them in foul trouble early. On the count of three, 'Heavy Hitters', ready, one, two, three,"

"Heavy Hitters!" they all yelled together.

"Okay, go warm up! Blacktop at its best people,"

"I'm DJ Baas,"

"And I'm DJ Qua."

DJ Baas continued, "And it's lights camera action tonight. We gotta show some love to Latifah, Shack, Wyclef and Method Man, came out to see two good teams go at it. Big ups to Brick City, Big Body Cadillac Club with Malik, the GM Club with my boy Greg. I can't forget Redline Bike Club, big ups to my dude, Nash. All last minute bets to the DJ booth." the DJ's spoke into the mic.

"Five minutes 'til tip-off! I expect 100 percent out there 'Heavy Hitters!' if you can't give me that keep yo' ass on the bench!" said Coach Jarell.

"Brick City women you ladies show and prove, lookin' good out here tonight. Let the show begin!"

The starting five of both teams came to the middle of the court for tip-off. 'Surprise' controlled the tip-off; TY got the ball for an easy lay-up for two. DJ Qua got the crowd amped up by putting on Beyoncé *'Crazy In Love'*; it blasted through the park!

Kaleem inbound the ball to Lil Dave to bring up the court; Lil Dave was moving up the court. Lil Dave hit Kaleem with the no look pass in the corner for three. At the other end, Smooth got the ball in the hole reverse and lays it in; Kaleem inbound to Na'eem. Na'eem tried to hit the baseline, but kicked it back out to Dave, he lobbed the ball to Ta'Rod and Ta'Rod caught the ball in the air and slammed it with one hand! Oh my God, the crowd went crazy! A couple of steals by 'Surprise' had done them well. *What a good game.*

It's Halftime, and 'Heavy Hitters' are down by ten, 'Surprise' is trying to run the score up on these guys.

"They workin' the hell out of you guys. Down low, the ref's ain't callin' shit, so don't look for the whistle at all. Ta'Rod you and Wali both got three fouls make them respect your jump shot, Wali, and if they come out, do the give and go, and move with the ball." Coach Jarell told them and went on to say, "We are only down by ten points. That ain't nothing. The score is 48-38. We can beat them! Let's go back out there this second half and go hard!"

"I taste a victory." Lil Dave said.

Their defense was tight down low, Lil Dave managed to get a bounce pass into Wali, and he made the short hook shot. Na'eem somehow ran down the loose ball that he knocked back to Wali.

"That's what I'm talkin' 'bout; movin' without the ball!" Coach Jarell yelled.

Na'eem got back up running down the court, Wali kicked it out to Lil Dave in the corner, Dave threw it to the top of the key to Na'eem– he pulled the three, and it was good!

"Now we ballin'," said Lil Dave. The whole park was on their feet. *Now that is how you hustle!*

"Time out!" Kaleem called after getting trapped.

Coach Jarell huddled up with the guys, "Way to go guys: this is what I want now, y'all goin' full court press! Who tired?"

"We good coach," Ta'Rod responded.

"Man-to-man here on out; call out who got who right now so everybody knows!"

"I got 12," said Ta'Rod.

"Give me 53," Kaleem joined in.

"I'ma take 7," said Na'eem.

"I got 31 all day," Wali spoke up.

"23 is all mine," said Dave.

Lil Dave had the ball in his hands. 'Surprise' don't want to foul this guy, he is like ninety percent from the line! 'Surprise' got man-to-man defense with forty-nine seconds left on the clock. With the score sixty-two to sixty, Lil Dave took the ball between his legs and tried to come off the tight pick set by Na'eem. 'Surprises' center stepped up and canceled that thought. Lil Dave took the ball back to the top; he signaled Wali and Ta'Rod to take their man out the paint. Lil Dave took two hard dribbles forward with his man backing him up. The clock began to run down; the crowd started the countdown; five, four... Lil Dave crossed his man to the right the crowd yelled two... Dave took two steps back and pull the three-pointer, and it's good! The crowd reached decibels like never before.

"This is blacktop at its best!" DJ Baas announced. Sixty-two to sixty-three, the players gave everyone a show tonight!

Soon as the game was over, Lil Dave went straight to his girl. And, Cladia had been checking out Kaleem the whole game. Cladia was a Japanese chick mixed with black; nice curves, long black hair that she wore in a neatly pulled back ponytail– she fucked with Mo from the Spyers.

Cladia knew Mo's partner Button, was around and she would get her ass kicked if anyone saw her up in Kaleem's space. *"Fuck it,"* she said to herself. *"I'ma at least hug him, with his fine ass."* She had on a white silk sundress, some nice sandals to match showing her freshly polished, pretty pedicured toes; her body was looking right in all the right places. *She was beautiful.* She walked up to Kaleem,

"Kaleem," she told him reaching in giving him a hug, while at the same time grabbing his penis in a hand, discreetly.

"What's good?" he responded, recalling that she was Mo's girl. From the corner of his eye, he saw Queen walking up to him, and spent off putting all his attention on Queen hoping she didn't see much.

"Is that his girl?" Queen thought.

"Hi, my Queen," he turns to her to greet her.

Cladia stood there with a dumb look on her face and didn't like it one bit. Cookie gave Cladia the, bitch don't get ya' ass beat out here today look, and then adjusted the razor blade she always carried in her mouth; she called them the 'bitch act right razors'.

"Hi Kaleem, I hope I didn't disturb anything?" Queen said as she and her friend approached, taking a glance at Cladia as she walked off.

"Nah, hell no; how long y'all been here?"

"Ten minutes into the first quarter. Kaleem, this is my friend, Cookie." They both greeted each other, and Queen went on to say, "I see you got a little game, although you can work on ya' left more." she said in a playful manner.

"What you know about ballin', beautiful?"

"I'm a Lakers fan, ever since Magic! The best NBA team," she boasted.

"So you a Kobe fan?"

"Yes, sir, I can say y'all played hard out there."

"How do y'all keep these guys off y'all back?" he asked her.

"We tell them we're gay."

"What?"

"Yeah, that'll get them off us faster than a New York minute," said Cookie.

"Look how y'all look, you can't blame them; they know beauty when they see it," Kaleem said.

"No, they want booty," Cookie replied.

"Well maybe that too," Kaleem agreed.

"I just wanted to see if you had game or not," Queen stated.

"So what you think?"

"You aight," she said jokingly.

Kaleem laughed, "I'ma let you get that."

"You know, I know Queen Latifah, and her mom is giving a Cancer Awareness benefit next month in West Orange. Let me know if you want to attend." Queen told him.

"That's What's Up."

"Well, let me know, the tickets are fifty dollars. You ready to go, Cookie?"

"Yep,"

"Well, Mr. Kaleem, we're about to hit Short Hills Mall…"

"No Girl, Jersey Garden, they close at eleven tonight." Cookie replied interrupting.

"Can I hit you up later tonight?" Kaleem asked Queen.

"Sure, that's fine."

"Nice meeting you Cookie,"

"Same here, peace my brother,"

"I'll walk y'all to ya' car; don't want these hounds all over y'all. Where you park at?"

"Cookie double parked right over here," Queen responded pointing.

"Queen here is a few dollars to grab you some extra stuff from the mall."

"No thank you, my momma told me about what men expect when you take money."

"My mom's ain't told me shit! I'll take it." Cookie said with sass.

"Nah, Queen, it's not like that,"

"It's cool, but thanks anyway."

"Call me," Kaleem said, giving Queen a hug before she got in the car.

"Later." Cookie said and pushed the gas.

As soon as they pulled off... Baca! Baca! Baca! Shots were let off inside the park. People started screaming and running in all directions; tumbling over one another, and falling everywhere.

Kaleem immediately got down, took his phone out, and called Moose to check on everyone, "What the fuck is going on!" he yelled into the phone when Moose answered.

"Kaleem you in front of the park?" Moose asked, breathing heavily through the phone.

"Yeah,"

"You got a guy with dreads and a black duffle bag, burn his ass! Don't let him go!" Moose said indignantly!

Kaleem started walking towards the guy with the dreads and pulled his .40-caliber from under his towel. The guy was running and looking back to see if anyone was running behind him; when he turned back around, he bumped into Kaleem.

Bam! Bam! Bam! "Take those free of charge," Kaleem told him after hitting him with three bullets to the chest.

Ta'Rod pulled up as o-boy fell to the street. Kaleem hoped in the car, "Drive!" he said, throwing his hand in a forward motion.

"You good?" Moose asked Kaleem still on the phone with his hand to his Bluetooth, securing it.

"Yeah, I'm straight. What about y'all?"

"Everybody good,"

"What happened?"

"O-boy and his two partners were jackin' niggas in the park, they fucked up when they tried to get Lil Dave's necklace. Two of 'em got hit up in the park. O-boy with the bag ran— that's the one you served up!"

"Yo', my forty flat-lined his ass!" Kaleem stated, nodding his head up and down looking at his piece.

"I got to go the sirens getting close," Moose said.

"That's what it is; I got something for you later," Kaleem told Moose and then hung up.

"I felt some shit was gone jump off."

"You damn sure was right," Ta'Rod responded.

"Look at this," Kaleem said, looking in the black duffle bag he snatched from the dude with the dreads, "shit, phones, jewelry, money, tape, and handcuffs. Fuck 'em." he glanced at Ta'Rod then to his .40-Glock and began caressing it, "my girl right here…" he said, referring to his gun, "how I caressed her body that shit got me hard. That was my first time breakin' her in."

"Yo' ass is a fool, man."

"Make sure that three brick deal is set for in the morning," Kaleem said changing the subject.

"I got it covered."

"Wait, hold on... Hello," Kaleem said answering his phone.

"Hey, Kaleem, this is Queen. Are you all right? We heard them shooting. One of Cookie's friends called her and said it was a grisly scene; one guy's brains were splattered on the street, and blood was pouring out his eyes— it was a river of blood on the streets," she said frantically.

"Damn, nah I left right after y'all did."

"Well, that's good. Are you ok?" she asked.

"Yeah, I'm good. Thanks for checkin' on me," he told her and went on to say, "If you ever want to play one on one let me know,"

"If we do, I will spot you a few points," she said jokingly.

"Oh, no you didn't go there!" he said and they both laughed.

"Well, I was just calling to check on you. I'll get at you later."

"Okay." They disconnected the call.

"Yo', I'm gonna cop me another car," Kaleem told Ta'Rod.

"What you waiting on, joker?"

"I don't want nothing fancy— just something nice, feel me?"

"Nah, I ain't feelin' that. Go hard shit you only live once. They want us to think like that. I live for more people than just me. Money comes and money goes."

"Yeah, but don't let it rule your life, fam. I'ma bust at you tomorrow like a chopper, Ta'Rod." Kaleem said as they pulled up to his destination and got out the car.

KARIEM

"One love, get at me."

CHAPTER 12

Kaleem just brought him a brand new Honda Accord and was on his way to pick up some rims for it on Broadway at Shorty's Wheels, and then to Robbie so he can put some beat in it.

"Rasol, what's good man?" Kaleem greeted as he pulled up and got out at Shorty's Wheels.

"What's good, man? That's yo' new ride?"

"Yeah, aye Rasol, I need to know if those full-face rims in yo' window fit my car?"

"Yep, those will fit, they are twenty-twos. With everything thirty-five hundred, we talking."

"Can I pick it back up today?

"Fill out this paperwork and I will have it ready for you tomorrow."

"Okay, that's good. I'll be back then to pick it up." Kaleem told him as he saw Ta'Rod pull up to pick him up.

"That's what it is homie."

* * *

"Ta'Rod, we got to talk."

"Get in. What's up?" he asked.

"I got a call last night that it was Black and his team robbed ya' spot on twenty-first and Hopkins,"

"What?"

"They don't want you taking their people. We got the best cocaine around and they hatin' hard, feel me?"

"That ain't goin' down like that." Ta'Rod agreed. "The wolves never get any sleep. They always plotting to come at ya', promise that, my nigga. They want you to feed 'em."

"That's the truth, word is bond. Hold on while I call Hassan."

"Yo', who this?" Hassan answered.

"It's Kaleem, What good Hass?"

"My bad, how you doin', Kaleem? This damn girl talkin' shit to me again, 'cause I ain't come by last night. She either wants Mr. Good-bar or not," they both laughed. "But on the real, what's up with ya'?"

"Our spot on Twenty-first got robbed a few weeks back,"

"Yeah, yeah, Black and his team, right?" Hass had already known. "You know the streets talk,"

"Well, I want to send the streets a message back that we ain't havin' it! Feel me?"

"I hear you. Now hear me, ten stacks can make it happen. Five up front and five after the hit,"

"Hold on while I tell Ta'Rod the business."

"Can he handle it?" Ta'Rod asked.

"Of Course, Yo' Hass I'ma get that to you today,"

"Get at me," Hass stated and then they hung up.

"Ta'Rod, run me on Court Street to drop some work off."

"Alright,"

Kaleem called Dawg, "Hey Dawg, this Kaleem, I will be at you in fifteen minutes."

"That's the business," Dawg responded and then hung up.

Ta'Rod and Kaleem bobbed their heads to DMX's *'What These Bitches Want'* as it played through the car speakers as they hit the 'Brick City' streets.

"So many beautiful women in 'Brick City' they show and prove. They put on for their city!" Kaleem said checking out his surroundings.

"They sure do," Ta'Rod agreed.

They pulled up to where Dawg was. "Yo', what's good fellas?" Dawg said as he got in the car.

"What's up with you?" Kaleem asked. "I had to get a re-up. Somebody caught them in New Community slippin' last night smokin' drinkin' and playin' ce-low. Three got hit up."

"Damn. I got twenty-seven,"

"Okay, take these four,"

"That's good lookin'. I'ma holla at y'all be easy, one love." Dawg said as he bounced.

"Ta'Rod, take me to handle this money with Hass,"

"Yeah, 'cause, I want to get that out the way,"

"One day I want to retire from this shit, be like my girl Assata Shakur and go chill in another country," Kaleem thought.

They made it to Leslie Street in no time. Ta'Rod pulled up and honked the horn. Hass walked up and got inside the car. "Peace, fellas," Hass greeted.

"What's up?" Ta'Rod and Kaleem both responded.

"Here is the five grand, Hass," Kaleem said, passing him the money.

"Five stacks!" Hass responded counting out the money.

"Handle your business," Ta'Rod replied.

"Kaleem, tell ya' man about me; I always take care of my handle. Just make sure that other half is in place once it's finished,"

"I got you covered," Kaleem answered.

"Alright, later,"

"Later," Kaleem said before they pulled off the block.

"Ta'Rod, you want to grab a sandwich from Bragman's Deli over on Hawthorne Avenue or DJ's on Irvine Turner Boulevard?"

"Hell yeah, they both make some big ass sandwiches,"

"Yeah, since we on this side of town, 'cause if not I would say let's hit Coopers! You know Newark got the line of police cars that be ridin' like fifteen deep jumpin' out on blocks searchin' and checkin' for ID."

"I know that's the train," Ta'Rod replied. As he was driving down Clinton Place, he noticed a black Caprice was tailing them; it was the police for sure. Ta'Rod hit the gas, bust a couple of turns and it was a wrap; they lost them. "I got to park this car like now, fuck that food," he stated still looking in is rearview mirror.

"I'ma scream at you tomorrow, Ta'Rod,"

"Okay, bust at me like a chopper tomorrow," he replied and then pulled off.

* * *

Kaleem picked up his Honda from Shorty's Wheels today; he was in the game now. As he cruised the streets, it seemed like everybody was eyeing his new shiny rims. The rims on his Honda had the car looking right. The voices were back in his head; it was like the good fighting the bad.

Kaleem rolled down Seventh Street by Avon. "Oh Shit!" he said as two detective cars boxed him in.

The detectives jumped out their cars with their guns drawn on Kaleem as they approached both sides of his car. "Kaleem!" Robo Cop yelled, tapping his gun on the drivers' window.

"Turn the fucking car off!" the other detective told him from the passenger side.

"Put your fucking hands on the steering wheel where we can see them!" Robo Cop said and then snatched the door open. "You and ya' boy Ta'Rod thought that was cool the other day, he can drive pretty good," he told him and went on to say, "anyway this the deal, y'all gonna start breaking us off. Or else we're gonna shut yo' asses down!"

"I don't know what you talkin' about,"

"I'ma headache and an asshole too," the detective on the drivers' side said. "So think about what I said," he told him and then slammed the door.

After they left, Kaleem hit up with Ta'Rod and told him what was going on.

"His ass needs to be put in a box," Ta'Rod said to Kaleem after he told him about his encounter with the two detectives.

"Nothin' is gonna stop this cash flow, they gone need the FBI and CIA! Feel me?"

"That's what's up,"

"Yo', I'ma get at you. I'm goin' by Ben's Barbershop to scream at Kenny and Lionel to see if they want to shoot some pool tonight,"

"I'll meet you over there. I need to holla' at Bobe."
"That's what it is, peace." They both hung up.

CHAPTER 13

Channel 2 News was doing a special report on car thieves.

"Buddy-Love is one of Newark cops enemy's because the fact he is a professional car thief. Why do you steal cars?" the news reporter stated and then asked Buddy-Love.

"The danger that comes with it, the cops shooting, killing yourself, running someone over or getting caught, the plus side is the money, to prove that there ain't no car that I can't get, and I'm the best at what I do, what a rush!" Buddy-Love said to the Channel 2 CBS News reporter. "My name ring bells around here, that's why you gave me a stack to do this interview. I'ma give y'all a show, trust me! Hold on let me tie this shirt over my face." He took out a t-shirt and tied it around his face. "Now you can roll the camera. Yeah, keep drivin' we are almost in Hillside right next to Newark. Ok, pull over right here," he told him as they passed The White Castle on Elizabeth Avenue. "Wait in the parking lot right there, when you hear the sirens that's how you'll know the show is on!"

"Okay, I got ya'." said Bill the camera operator.

"C'mon, let me out!" Buddy-Love said as he saw a black Porsche 944 sitting near Route 22 Honda's dealer. "If I'm gonna be on TV I gotta profile and style."

Buddy-Love pulled out a five-pound snatch bar and a flat head screwdriver. He took the snatch bar, broke the park light lens, and grounded out the alarm inside the socket of the bulb. He pried into the keyhole of the driver door and connected the two wires leading to the keyhole to jump two wires, making the door locks jump. Once he was in, he pulled twice on the ignition with the snatch bar and put the screwdriver inside the ignition– Vroom! And there you had it, the Porsche was started!

"I am damn good!" he said to himself. *"Now, let's get this shit jumpin'!"*

He drove the borderline of Grumman Avenue, getting the attention of a Newark and a Hillside police car with his mask on his face. He held the brakes and pressed the gas burning out in front of them. "Fuck the police, it's on!" the police got behind him and was on his tail.

The sixteen-inch Pirelli tires made love to the streets as he hauled ass. He came past Elizabeth Towers blowing the horn doing fifty, ready to hit the brakes just in case they got too close. He let them hit him in the back, making their airbags come out. The TV crew saw him coming up White Castle doing sixty. He locked his emergency brakes, cut the wheel hard to the left drifting into the intersection.

"Oh shit!" he yelled out, as the car was turning hard to the left. He tapped the brakes to get the Porsche back the way he needed it. "Damn, I'm good!" he blurted out in excitement.

Inside the intersection of Hawthorne and Elizabeth Avenue, he started doing donuts. He locked the cruise button in place and sat his ass out the window holding the wheel with one hand and smacking his ass with the other, giving his grand finale. It was so much smoke couldn't nobody see anything. All the police could do was just look and be amazed at the driving skills of whoever was behind the wheel of the Porsche. Two o'clock in the afternoon, that was some action for 'Brick City'. After roughly three minutes, you couldn't hear the tires from the Porsche screaming anymore. It was like a magic trick when the white smoke cleared, the black Porsche was gone! No doubt, this kid is one of the best.

CHAPTER 14

Clinton Avenue, Elizabeth Avenue and McCarter Highway was all jumping with prostitution, the street level to the upper-class— people chasing a piece of new ass.

Some pimp name Pretty Ricky had a team of girls and when he started putting under age thirteen and fourteen-year-old girls on the strolls with their adult developed bodies and six-inch heels, the old men were all over them. The cops had picked him up three times, but the girls never told on him so they let him go every time.

When the pimp 'Mike The Dike' saw the young girls, he knew he had to see Pretty Ricky. That crazy shit just didn't sit right with him.

Summertime cookouts swim parties, guys, girls, trucks, cars, and money; the smell of rubber from so many burnouts. The Nitrous in the air that made anything fly. It's Saturday night live down in the Hole between Badger and Peshine Avenue.

A dude from Hemingway, South Carolina name Elias towed his shining red Ford Mustang. Pumping a booming 540 horsepower supercharged motor. He is going to be racing Kaleem with his racecar, an M3 BMW with a V8 engine 520 horses shooting nitro. Bets were stacking up. Everyone knew it would be a hell of a race. Both drivers will put up twenty thousand dollars apiece. And with the spectators the purse can be one hundred thousand dollars or better.

"I'm gonna stop you from coming up here chasin' this 'Brick City' cash," Kaleem said.

"That's the only reason I keep comin' up here," said Elias. "Plus I love the action!"

"Check this out bro, we got money for years, long money, and we don't care about spendin' it 'cause we make it. Feel me?"

"I hear you talkin' Kaleem."

"Any time you got ballers, you have a gorgeous woman around as well."

"Now you damn sure right about that, Kaleem," they both laughed.

Linda was rolling in her 420 Benz to go grab a bite to eat. Kaleem spotted her through the crowd around the Hole and gave her a wave to pull over. She rolled down her tinted windows... "Hi, Mr. Kaleem," she spoke, letting everyone see how beautiful she was.

"I knew that was your car. How are you doing, Linda?"

"I'm good,"

"That you are, baby,"

That statement placed a smile on her face, knowing, that it was the truth. She was a beauty, butter pecan complexion, curly black Indian hair, large breast, and a heart shaped behind.

"You stay too busy for a sister,"

"Nah, honey, that's not the case. I'ma call you tonight."

"I'm going to bed early. I'm going to Asbury Park with my sisters tomorrow morning. I know I won't get any sleep if you come by tonight and I'm drivin' us down!"

"Well, call me when you get back because you're right!"

"Okay, I'll do that."

Kaleem reached in the car and gave her a kiss. "Don't start nothing you can't finish, Mr. Kaleem." She tastes as sweet as she looked all eyes were on them. Everyone looked as she said goodbye looking very sexy with her Gucci shades on.

"Damn, yo', where you find her at?" Bones asked as AB walked up.

"I know she got friends," AB stated.

"Of course, it's a few of them that roll together."

"We need to get together with them," Bones suggested.

"Word," AB agreed.

Vroom… Vroom! Two bikes pulled up that took the conversation over, a hot Suzuki Hayabusa, blue and chromed out.

"How about the Kawasaki 1200 with the Wolverine paint job," Kaleem said.

The riders parked and turned off their bikes. A few people walked over to check out the guys leather down on the nice bikes. They were looking to race. However, experience bikers pay attention when a racer never takes his helmet off to expose who they are. You could be trying to beat an AMA Pro American Superbike racer out catching a sucker! Both bikes were set for racing Air-shifters, power packs and nitrous.

"Bones you and AB comin' to watch the cars tonight?"

"Yeah, Hope you can handle what's on ya' plate," Bones replied.

"Those superchargers fly," AB said.

"My car will do what it do. My boy at Northern State prison, said they lookin' for a good race also. There go Reese he just copped that white 500 Mercedes, it got the AMG package shit that's about one fifty."

"That dog food keeps his safe packed."

Mike The Dike, the OG pimp rolled through in his black Caddy. Everybody knew he kept some official beautiful women on his team. He didn't stop, he kept it moving up Clinton Avenue, towards Eighteenth Street.

"Dawn." The Dike said to one of his girls. "Listen, I gotta show that 'Pretty Ricky' cat that his career is over in "Brick City" once and for all. He looks for these runaway young girls, feed 'em drugs and get them hooked on his bullshit feel me?"

"Yes, I do," Dawn replied.

"They are young and gullible. I am confident that once he meets you he will be inspired to put you on his team. Once you are effective in doing that then he will learn the difference in a grown as woman!"

"Speaking of Ricky, look," Hassana said as she is driving. "There is his Lexus, parked on Twentieth Street," she stated, pointing.

"You're right," The Dike said. "Keep drivin' to the carwash right by there. Dawn, you can walk back over there do what you do and call me when you got something for me."

"Ok, Daddy, I got you," Dawn replied and got out the Caddy. Dawn is a head turner, golden brown skin, with black short hair. Women would die for her body. A superstar; wearing her gold and black Kenneth Cole body dress with gold matching pumps and a large Coach bag;

women always checked Dawn out. She had so much style about herself. Her class demanded attention!

Pretty Ricky saw Dawn half a block away. *"Damn,"* he thought as he keeps adjusting his eyes on her body and face. "Hello beautiful," he stated.

"Hi," she replied.

"Yo' you lookin' for me?" he asked her.

"I'm workin' makin' money; you got enough?" she said.

"Listen, bitch, I'm a pimp, I don't pay for shit. I got tricks working for me. If you act right, I might make somethin' outta ya' ass."

"Here you go, Ricky, I got your money," one of his girls said as she walked up.

"See what I'm talkin' bout?" Pretty Ricky said. "This Lisa, she's never short on my cash, she got locked up in Greene Street for three days until they found out she was fourteen. I can't loose with these young bitches. Young and fresh that's all the old men want these days. So I keep 'em supplied."

As the sun was setting, the traffic was getting heavy on Eighteenth Street. "Lisa go get me a bottle of water, a pack of Black and Mild's, and a pack of Newport's."

"I'll walk with her," said Dawn.

"Yeah, you do that while I think about forgivin' you for that shit that came out ya' mouth."

"What's good, Lisa? I'm Dawn. How are you, girl? Lisa, girl how long have you been working now?"

"Three weeks, no, it's a little over a month now. I'ma hate when the winter gets here." they laughed.

"Where is your family?"

"Well, I kind of don't have a family. I left my house because my mom's boyfriend would molest and rape me all the time. Mommy didn't believe me when I told her. So I went to stay with my Aunt Irene in North Newark on Mt. Prospect Avenue. I did what I wanted to over there, and then I met Pretty Ricky while buying some pizza. He paid for it and took me shopping, and I never went back to my Auntie house. I don't like when they are mean and rough, they be having me sore, and Ricky still makes me go out to work the block. I have nowhere else to go," Lisa said sadly.

Beep, beep,

"That's him blowing for me don't say anything, please."

"I won't."

"Get in!" Pretty Ricky yelled.

Dawn kept thinking of what Lisa had just told her. Surely, Lisa was afraid of him.

Pretty Rickey pulled up to the Motor Lodge Motel in Irvington. Wait here while I go get a room. *"I'ma show Dawn how I work this dick,"* he said to himself laughing, getting out the car.

As soon as he got out the car, Dawn texted The Dike,

IRV Motor Lodge, now!

"I hate when he wants sex. He has a small dick so he uses a twelve-inch strap on. I guess to feel like he is doing something. Here he comes," Lisa said.

"C'mon, let's go inside so we can have a good time," he told them.

Dawn dropped a Big Red gum wrapper by the room door to let The Dike know what room they were in just in case she couldn't use her phone again. Dawn was sharp and on point. The motel was low budget, a full-size bed an old TV bolted to the wall in room 34.

Soon as they walked in, he closed the door, locked it, and punched Dawn dead in her mouth, knocking her to the floor. Lisa ran straight into the bathroom, afraid that she would be next. He slapped her around continuously. "Bitch who in the hell you think you fuckin' with? You gonna work them streets for me like the rest of them." Dawn tried to block the blows she was receiving to her face.

He grabbed her Coach bag and emptied it on the bed going through it; he took the two hundred dollars she had. "You won't need this money; I'll take care of all you need from now on. Get yo' ass up," he demanded. "I got some ecstasy and twelve-inches of dick for you."

Dawn got up grabbing her bag, putting the items back inside. "You with that fake ass bag, I'll buy you a real one if you can sell enough pussy!" Pride is the most fundamental of the seven deadly sins and he owns this false pride! "Go clean yo' ass up so the party can start."

"Lisa is in the shower," she said. The whole time Dawn was being slapped and punched around Lisa was in the shower hoping by the time she got out everything would be cooled down.

"Are you aight?" Lisa inquired, coming out the bathroom. "He likes to knock us around too," she whispered.

"I'm good. Can you stay in here while I get myself together?" Dawn asked.

"Girl go ahead, he looks at porn and pop those pills before he ready to have sex."

Knock, Knock, Knock,

"Who is it?" Pretty Ricky said.

"It's the front desk. Someone left a package for this room," the voice on the other side of the door answered.

"What fuckin' package? Leave it at the door!" Ricky lived an out of control life. When he was a child, his father went through a lot of mental and physical abuse. He went to the United States Army in 1945 returning from the battlefield of Europe and defeating Hitler, only to come back to the States to decimation and racial violence. His father, John turned his problems to heroin. He would beat Pretty Ricky, burn him with fire, and would lock him in a dark closet for days at a time. The trauma caused Pretty Ricky to be on Prozac, Thorazine, and Tegretol® medication. From there he went to heroin, coke, and ecstasy; at times being very confused.

"What the hell is this?" Pretty Ricky said as he opened the door and saw a bag with a shoebox filled with dirt and a bottle of honey. *Somebody playing games; I guess they had the wrong room on some freaky shit."* Pretty Ricky thought.

"Lisa, when we go in there I want you to turn the TV volume up as loud as it will go," Dawn said.

"Why?" Lisa questioned.

"Because I got something for his ass," Dawn pulled the bottom of her Coach bag apart, pulling out a compact Taurus nine-millimeter automatic. "I'm not letting him get away with the shit he has been doin!"

"Bring y'all ass out that fuckin' bathroom!" he yelled in a demanding tone.

"You do what I said, alright."

"Okay." Lisa agreed and they walked out the bathroom.

Lisa walked out first went straight to the television and turned the volume up as high as it would go.

"You stupid bitch!" Pretty Rickey jumped up and slapped the shit out of Lisa. "What the fuck do you think you doing?"

Boom!

Dawn shot Pretty Ricky in the right thigh. He hit the floor and looked to see Dawn holding her gun to his head. "Open your mouth you son of a Bitch!" Dawn was in control. He did as she said not wanting Dawn to make any crazy moves and shot him again. She shoved a pair of socks in his mouth. Lisa was shocked at what just happened. *Pretty Ricky was no longer in control.* Ricky had already taken off all his clothes and was naked.

"Lisa, get the bed sheet." Lisa hurried to grab the sheet from the bed. "Get the fuck on the bed!" Dawn yelled. "Lisa takes the knife he has in his pocket and rip the sheet up so we can tie his ass up."

Lisa tied Ricky's arms and legs. Just like Dawn said. His eyes were bloodshot red. He had the anger of a lion inside a pack of sheep! He wondered how he'd missed Dawn having a gun with her. The ecstasy pills had him feeling some kind of way. Lisa hauled off and hit him in the face with everything she had, causing his nose to bleed. His sounds were muzzled from his mouth being stuffed. Lisa was filled with enthusiasm from the way Dawn took control.

Dawn leaned over Pretty Ricky's ear and said, "In your next life, make sure you respect the power of a woman, mother fucker!" Dawn looked around and saw Lisa putting on the strap on penis. Lisa took the twelve-inch penis put

Vaseline only on the head of it and forced every inch inside his rectum, in and out in and out until Lisa felt herself having an orgasm. Dawn was wet just looking at her actions. It was obvious he was inspired with pain.

Lisa pulled the fake penis out of him and the room filled with a terrible odor of shit! Blood came flowing out of his rectum. Lisa started crying because her conscious allowed her to reminisce about all the men and things Pretty Ricky would make her do.

Dawn gave her a hug. "Get right, it's over now girl," she told her.

Pretty Ricky finally felt the pain of agony that he made the girls go through for so long with his control and sickness. Dawn grabbed the sweet honey from the bag and began to rub it all over his body from head to toe. She then took the box of dirt and shook the dirt over every part of his body. Emerging from the dirt was over one million Red Tiger Ants. They were hungry for the honey and blood! Bites, bites, and more bites. He felt every step the ants would take over his body and every time they would bite into his skin. They made holes in his body creeping inside the flesh. They were coming in and out of everywhere, eyes, nose, ears, mouth, penis, and anal; they made their own super highway. He was fighting to get loose; he knew this was the end of his career. The ants came together like an army and continued to eat Ricky alive. *What a way to die.* The ants were broadcasting signals to each other while releasing formic acid within his skin. He became weaker and weaker as his vision faded away. Dawn made sure the slug from the bullet did not lodge inside the wall or floor. She turned on the shower and allowed the moisture from the steam to cover the room, and then began wiping their prints off everything.

Dawn leaned over Ricky's moribund body and said, "Now who got fucked? You're the bitch now! Go to hell!" Both girls looked at the dead body smiled and left the motel room.

* * *

Two a.m. 70-degree dry and hot weather the same night, a huge crowd of people was out to watch the race. Cars, trucks and bikes all parked on the side of Interstate highway 78 by Northern State prison. Four SUVs got behind the starting line to wait for the signal to block off the highway. Elias got his Mustang off the trailer. Guys poured bleach on the ground, allowing the two drivers to heat up their tires with a short burn-out. Both drivers were told to line up. It was about to go down! The SUVs turned on their Hazard lights, letting everyone know the highway is blocked off bringing traffic to a standstill. The flagman asked both drivers were they ready. They nodded simultaneously *"yes!"*

The flag had dropped. The cars pulled off evenly, the BMW jumped ahead of the Mustang by a car length. Kaleem was fighting to straighten his car back out because he had shot more nitrous causing his car to fishtail. Elias supercharger kicked in and his Mustang flew pass the BMW winning by a car length. 110 mph in the quarter mile run, *what a good race!*

All the specters all jump in their vehicles to meet back at the Hole…

"Damn, Kaleem, what the hell happened?" Super Kool asked.

"I hit the juice again and almost lost the car. By the time I got it straight Elias was comin' pass me,"

"There he is now," Super Kool stated, pointing.

"Shot too much gas Kaleem?" Elias asked being funny.

"That's why you won, don't get it twisted. Let's go back for fun, for forty thousand apiece,"

"My Mustang needs work done,"

"Nah, you just don't wanna lose yo' cash. I got another fifty grand and I'll spot you with my GTO," Super Kool boasted.

"Make that seventy thousand," said Mark.

"Maybe next time," Elias said wisely.

"I know you not stupid," someone in the crowd said.

"You're still a winner to me," Sharon told Kaleem. "Can you come over tonight?"

"I want to, but I got to put my car up,"

"Well, just call me if you change your mind,"

"That's what it is, baby,"

"Good race," Kaleem told Elias as they shook hands. "Have a safe trip back home, hurry back, I got something for your ass," Kaleem told him.

"C'mon you know I'll be back," Elias responded, throwing his hands in the air turning to leave.

"Damn, I got to have that nitrous adjusted better than that. I got him next time." Kaleem thought to himself.

"Damn, Kaleem, you buying some outfits from me tomorrow?" Jabrell asked.

"Shit didn't you bet with o-boy with the Mustang?"

"Hell nah, don't play me like that, I lost a hundred dollars on yo' ass,"

"Just checkin',"

"Here's two hundred. I should have won!"

"Yo' good lookin' Kaleem,"

"I'ma get at ya' Jabrell,"

"Peace homie."

* * *

"Oh my God!" the maid said as she opened the door to the motel room. Seeing the body and the odor almost made her faint. She ran to tell the manager. "Oh my God! Oh my God! A... A... Room 34..." She couldn't even get it all the way out she was so panicked. "It's a dead body!" she finally got it out.

"A what!" He screamed out. He grabbed his phone and ran straight to the room. As soon as he walked in the room, he started shaking and dialed 911. Within ten minutes, homicide detectives and police were all over the place.

"Damn!" Detective Greene said when he saw the body on the bed. Ants were still feasting and crawling all over Ricky's body. Everyone that saw the body was devastated.

"I have never seen anything like this, even in the movies," said Detective Murray.

"He has no skin on his body. What could a person have done to be tortured like this?" stated Green.

"After thirty years on the force, I have never seen anything like this in my life," said Murray.

After being there for over three hours, everyone was still in shock of the gruesome discovery.

"Whoever this guy pissed off wanted him bad. Two prostitutes couldn't have done this," said Murray.

Hazmat suits had to be worn by the coroner to scoop the dead body into the bag. Channel 7 and Channel 2 was on top of it. The Headlines and News specials stated, **"Man tortured and killers still running loose!"** The heat was on.

CHAPTER 15

Nineteenth Street stayed getting money. They kept a tight set-up; gunmen were ready to bust their guns; no running up to cars at all. A smoker/crack head was pushing a shopping cart filled with all kinds of things, bottles, cans, clothes, metal, and garbage. You could smell this guy's odor just walking by him.

"What's up with ya' man?" Jackie asked. "I see you are new around here, you get high don't you?"

"Yeah, but I got to get some money, I'm broke."

You couldn't tell that Jackie got high because she looked good and stayed fly. Medium build, brown sugar skin and had respect. "I'm Jackie. Who are you?"

"Hawk,"

"Okay, Hawk, I got a spot where we can go get high and you can wash. You need some damn clothes. Just 'cause you get high don't mean you just give up. I'm just saying."

"Yeah, yeah, I feel ya'", Hawk replied.

They both walked down the street to the brown house where people went to get high.

Knock, Knock,

"Who is it?" a man's voice mumbled from behind the door.

"It's Jackie,"

"Hey, Jackie," Bill said as he opened the door.

"What's up?"

"Hey, Jackie," Barbra said. "Don't start running your mouth, Bill, you high as hell!

"Not yet," Bill responded, putting a rock of crack on the stem. You could see the thick cloud of white smoke rushing into Bill's lungs through his glass pipe. After three minutes Bill began to speak, "Now that was a blast. What you and your friend got for me?" he asked Jackie.

"Don't I always take care of you?" Jackie answered.

"I know that's right, especially bringin' company!"

"Shut up Bill! Here you go." Jackie told him, giving him two caps of coke. "Here you go, Hawk," She gave him two vials of coke that was cooked already.

No one asked about Hawk and no one cared. The apartment was filled with drug paraphernalia, pipes, screens, razors, burnt spoons, lighters, and baking soda. If you weren't getting high or tricking you couldn't just chill. No one sat by Hawk because of the way he smelled.

"Damn," Hawk said after blowing the smoke of crack out of his mouth.

"You got that I bet!" Jackie said.

"Yeah, this is some good shit!"

Jackie began to get an attitude because the drug dealers were calling her a tease. She wore the best clothes, she would boost everything she needed and was good at it. Hawk had chained and locked his pushcart outside as if he had to worry about someone stealing it. Bill got high and started putting people out the house. It was almost 12 a.m., they had no more money or coke, it was a wrap! Bill knew not to do Jackie like that; she would stop by just to give him food or coke for nothing. That made her be very important to Bill.

"Bill I'ma chill until the morning and Hawk is with me," Jackie said.

"You know you good, girl,"

"Thanks,"

"Jackie, I'ma go outside for a few," Hawk told her.

"Don't play no games with them out there. Wadoo found a stash, smoked it up, and then had the nerve to come back around. Well, they beat him down with a baseball bat.

"I promise I won't look for a stash."

A gray and maroon Caddy had pulled up and parked as Hawk was walking down the block. It was Black. Black was known for getting money and shooting people, he was heartless; a huge Suge Knight type of dude. He dapped the guys standing outside the building, "Yo' I got a pair of jumper cables for sale."

"What you want for them?" one of the guys said.

"Twenty," Hawk answered.

"Take this dime and get out my face!" Hawk took the dime and made his way back to Bill's house."

Knock, Knock,

"Who is it?"

"Hawk, I'm with Jackie,"

"C'mon in," Bill said as he opened the door. "Jackie, it's Hawk."

Hawk went to the bathroom and took a quick wash up. The odor was tamed some. "Here you go, Jackie, I got two nickels of cook-up.

"So you came up, huh?"

"It's a little something,"

"How long can you hold the smoke in your mouth, Hawk?"

"What makes you ask something like that?"

"I'll show you. Hold on while I use the bathroom," she said.

Jackie came back into the room; she had a washcloth with soap all over it. "Lay back on the bed."

Hawk did as she asked. Jackie unzipped his pants; pulled his penis out and washed him off. Her actions were making Hawk's manhood grow.

"Damn, Hawk, you're holdin' like the FBI!"

"I get it from my father, he was a pipe layer," Hawk said with a smile.

"I bet he was," she agreed. "Here baby, put this hit on your stem,"

Hawk puts the flame of fire to the pipe, and Jackie began to suck on his penis. His eyes grew big from the pleasure he was enduring.

"Mmm, he is the best." Jackie thought. A vacuum cleaner had nothing on her lungs.

As Hawk began to climax, he blew out a cloud of white smoke. Jackie was finger fucking herself at the same time making herself orgasm. Hawk nearly filled Jackie's mouth up when he exploded into her mouth.

"Hum, huh, damn you did that, baby!" Hawk said.

"That's what I call a body blast," Jackie said.

"I want to fuck you now,"

"Nah, it won't be any of that," Jackie replied, waving her pointer finger from side to side.

"What? I'm straight,"

"That is too much dick for me. Get some rest if you staying."

Hawk fell asleep and woke up to find Jackie had gone and left a note that read,

Had to bounce take care; here is five bucks I don't cook breakfast, LMAO! Jackie.

Hawk hung around thinking about Jackie all day; how sexy she looked in her skinny leg Baby Phat Jeans. He had been making store runs for the dealers and would yell 5-0 if the police rode by. He was looked at as a crack head bum.

Nighttime hit with its darkness. Jackie hadn't been by all day it was already 11:30 p.m. at night. Hawk was still thinking about the body blast that she had given him. *"Back to earth."* he thought.

Hawk heard the music pumping through the system of Black's Caddy. When Black got out his car, Hawk walked up to him, "Hey, you gotta dollar you can spare."

Bam! Black punched Hawk in the mouth, knocking him two feet backward. Hawk put his hand up to his mouth to catch the blood; the blood was leaking on the ground. Everyone was waiting for Black's next move.

"Don't you ever walk up on me like that again! Get the fuck from by me, you stink bastard!"

Hawk sat on the sidewalk and did nothing.

When Black went inside the building, a smoker name, Gale went over to Hawk. "I see you met Black. What up? I remember you were with Jackie."

"Have you seen her today?" he asked.

"Nah, Jackie don't come around a lot. Talk to you later, I'm goin' to make money on the Avenue."

"Later," Hawk replied.

"Black don't know what he got comin'," Hawk thought.

It was 12 a.m. and Black hadn't come out yet. The dealers were getting relaxed— smoking that exotic weed, Hydro, 189th, and Purp.

Standing in the hallways were two of the dealers. "Don't come up this bitch if you ain't got no money wit' ya' stink ass!" one stated with force.

"I got money, I got money," Hawk responded.

When Hawk's hands came out his pockets, he was pointing two .40-caliber Smith & Wesson's at them.

"Take it easy man," one said scared to death.

"Put all that shit in this bag!" Hawk had stripped them of all their dope, jewelry, and money. "Turn y'all pockets inside out and lay on the floor."

"Aight, aight, we doin' it,"

Hawk searched both and found a loaded 357 magnum; a smile came across his face.

Hawk heard the apartment door close upstairs, heavy footsteps, and Black talking on his phone. When Black turned for the next set of steps, he dropped his phone to reach for his gun at the sight of Hawk.

Bam! Bam! Hawk pumped two shots into Black laying him down. The two dealers bumped into each other in the doorway allowing Hawk to shoot both of them in the back. Hawk stepped over Black's huge body. "Remember me, bitch? Tell hell I sent you."

Bam! Hawk puts one in Black's forehead.

After getting Blacks gun, Hawk ran out of the building around the corner into the stolen Buick he had stolen. It was nobody around, no witnesses.

Jackie went to rehab to clean her act up, and never came back around. *Guess she just was trying to find her way in life.*

CHAPTER 16

Kaleem and Queen were on their way to the show in Atlantic City. The conversation within their two-hour ride there made it seem like he'd known her forever. The show was featuring Frankie Beverly and Maze, Toni Braxton, and Howard Hewitt.

Teddy Pendergrass played as they drove through the last tollbooth off the Garden State Parkway.

"I hope we have a good time tonight." Kaleem thought. As he looked over at Queen he thought, *"I can't wait to be up inside her. Damn, she looks sexy and fly."*

"Hello, Ma," Queen said as she answered her phone.

"How are you tonight," said Inez.

"Fine, I am in Atlantic City about to go to a concert with Kaleem,"

"That sounds beautiful. I think he is a sharp young man, tell him I said hello. And, whatever God does is for the best. I just want you to be happy, baby."

"I know Ma. I will be sure to tell him."

"You be safe and enjoy yourself."

"I will love you, Ma!"

"Love you too."

"My mom's said to tell you, whatever God does is for the best!"

"I agree with her," he responded and they both smiled.

They were finally inside the Caesars Hotel and Casino. It was nice, live; so many lights and people everywhere.

"Do you feel lucky tonight?" Kaleem asked Queen.

"Never gambled before,"

"Life is one big gamble,"

"You know what I'm saying?" she replied.

So much money was in the place. Security was everywhere; they covered the place like a comb. The mist of the breeze surrounded them. The Atlantic Ocean was beautiful with the stars shining off the water. People were chasing the American dream, the mighty dollar. Call girls were jumping in and out of Limos with their laptops and touch screens waiting for the next John to email or text. They were dressed to kill; no broke low budget women were around the joint. It was twenty-four hour around the clock gambling, ball 'til you fall. Slot machines neatly lined up with flashing lights to lure you in— some even being hundred dollar machines. They even had a lounge room for when your conscience humiliates you from losing everything you have and you want to cry with the rest of the losers. The servers were looking sexy showing so much skin...

"Excuse me, Miss," Kaleem said to one of the servers.

"Hello, sweetie, what can I help you with tonight? My Name is Nina."

"Well, Nina, we are from 'Brick City',"

"That's Newark right?" she asked.

"Yeah, you been there before?"

"I've been there a few times. What can I get you two?"

"I will have a double Hennessy no Ice and a Virgin Piña Colada for my Queen."

"Will that be all for now?"

"Yes, honey,"

"Okay, I'll be back in a few! By the way, I love ya' hair!"

"Thank you," Queen replied.

As Kaleem and Queen were waiting for the return of their drinks, they walked over to the cashier to buy some gambling chips. "How can I assist you tonight, Sir?" the cashier asked as they approached the window.

"Can I get a thousand dollars in fifty dollar chips, please?"

"Sure, here you are, Sir, good luck,"

Just as they approached the Black Jack table, the nice server came with their drinks. "Here you go," she said, passing Kaleem the drinks.

"You are a beautiful and pleasant lady. Thank you very much," he responded, passing Queen her drink and then giving her a twenty dollar tip.

"Thank you," said Queen. "I agree with him."

"Thank you." the waitress responded and walked away.

"You ready, Queen?" Kaleem asked as they sat at the Black Jack table.

"I never played this before,"

"You know how to count to twenty-one, right?"

"Of course, but…"

"No, but…"

The dealer is ready. "Hello," he greets checking out Queen.

"What's up?" Kaleem said firm to let him know she was with him.

"Please place all bets down," he said.

Kaleem put a hundred on his hand and five hundred on Queens. The first hand Queen had an ace of spades as her up card and a King of diamond in the whole. Kaleem had a king of hearts and a two of clubs. He needed a hit, which was a ten of diamonds. *Damn, he lost.*

Queen turned out Black Jack, the dealer had twenty; he gave her two purple chips. She was paid double, one thousand. "I'm not playing anymore; I don't want to lose your money."

"My money, that's yours, I lost my hand." He played a few more hands with no luck.

"You see what time it is," Queen said.

"You're right, we need to be making our way to the auditorium for the show. Let's go cash in your chips."

Queen looked like a super model, that didn't let her looks or body go to her head. She didn't know Kaleem wanted to wife her for life. Plus, she wasn't chasing his cash flow.

They had good seats thank God because the place was packed. The announcer took the stage. "Thank you, ladies and gentlemen, we are about to see and hear an exclusive show tonight. We have come for your pleasure, Toni Braxton, Frankie Beverly and Maze, and the man himself Howard Hewitt! I see you all need to give yourselves a round of applause!" The crowd began to make noise, clapping together and yelling. "So sit back and enjoy the show!"

Poof! A cloud of white smoke covered the stage. Toni Braxton stepped out waving hello and blowing, *"Love shoulda brought you, brought you, home last night you shoulda been with me Shoulda been right by my side…"*

The way she moved her body enhanced her emotions. You could feel her in your seat. Her next song *'Rapture'* made Kaleem think of how he wanted to be caught in Queen's *rapture*. After the curtain went down and came back up, Toni was in a white mini dress, singing, *"Seven Whole Days..."* The crowd was roaring with applause. That woman could sing no doubt!

"Kaleem, this is very nice. She can really sing,"

"I saw you and me when she sang *'Seven Whole Days.'*"

"Stop making me blush, Kaleem,"

"Real talk, you got me open."

The announcer screams into the crowd, "Frankie Beverly and Maze!" The audience was going wild; clapping for ten minutes before he could start to sing.

The words came through the sound system, *"You made me happy, this you can bet, you stood right beside me, yeah, and I won't forget. And I really love you, you should know, I wanna make sure I'm right, girl before I let go..."* Maze ripped it. Then came Howard with, *'This Is For The Lover In You...'* *"It's got to be real, girl, I could write a book on how you're makin' me feel, I know I'll never find another who could match the lovin' you've givin' to me..."*

"What a show!" Kaleem said.

"I really loved it," Queen replied.

"Queen, you know it's a two-hour ride and it's already 12:30 a.m., let's get a room and leave in the morning,"

"Getting a room is fine, but if you're expecting to have sex, that's out the question, Kaleem, I'm sorry," she said.

"Listen, I will never want anything that isn't for me. If and whenever you decide to, you will let me know."

"You are so sure of yourself, huh?" she asked with a hand on hip.

"I just know you are who I want. Do you want to grab a bit to eat?"

"It's up to you, Kaleem."

They went to the lobby of the Caesar's Palace and Kaleem paid for a luxury suite, one night's stay. The suite was nice; king size bed, kitchen, Jacuzzi, drinks, and two terry-cloth towels with their initials. That's the perks of a five-star hotel.

Room number 7, Kaleem slid the card across the lock. Soft jazz music was playing as they entered the room. The air was filled with the smell of fresh roses. The television was on CNN news.

The drive and the show had Kaleem a little worn out. He grabbed two cans of Red Bull and turned the water on full blast in the Jacuzzi adding bubbles. The heat was on this night.

Kaleem went to the bathroom to get comfortable. *"I hope she changes her mind."* he thought. When he came out the bathroom, Queen was already in the Jacuzzi.

"That looks like it feels good," he told her.

"It does."

Kaleem joined her; she still had on her bra and panties. He went up to her and wrapped his arms around her; she felt how excited he was from his erect penis. They both felt electricity through their bodies as he kissed her neck softly. Tears began to fall from Queen's eyes. As the tears flowed from her eyes, Kaleem sensed the agony of her pain. *But from what?* The amygdala of her brain, which is the seat of her emotions, had exploded at this time.

Queen got out the water, put her robe on, and sat on the couch crying. "What's wrong?" Kaleem asked, trying to comfort her.

"I'm dealing with a lot right now, I'm sorry. I just don't know. I didn't mean to mess up your night, Kaleem."

"I thought it was my cologne," he said, trying to get a smile out of her. "Get some rest. You will feel better in the morning, honey. They both laid down and fell asleep in each other's arm.

Kaleem woke up the next morning admiring how beautiful Queen was. The ride back to Newark was quiet. He didn't sex her like he wanted, but it will be a next time.

Home sweet home, Kaleem pulled up in front of Queen's place. "Thank you, Kaleem, for such a good time," she told him.

"Everything is good, we straight," he replied.

"Well, you can call me if we still cool," she told him. "Thanks again." She kissed him on the cheek and went inside.

CHAPTER 17

"It has been a month now since our trip to Atlantic City," Queen thought. *"How long could I go without having sex with him before he goes?"*

Knock, Knock,

"Who is it?" Queen asked, interrupted out her thoughts.

"Cookie, open the damn door, girl!" When Queen opened the door, Cookie marched straight in, "You ain't gonna believe this shit, girl."

"What?"

"Omar called himself being slick getting us a supporter, right?"

"Yeah,"

"Girl, the nigga didn't tell me. I know his son need shit, I need shit and he needs shit. If o-girl can foot the bill, then more power to her ass. Anyway, the bitch name is Tracy. Now she had the nerve to call my phone talkin' shit to me, right. So I made Omar take me over there to the bitch house. She didn't come outside, so I stabbed his ass three times for not tellin' me!

"Girl, you crazy,"

"I been knew that," Cookie agreed. "He only had to get a few stitches, he lucky! Yo' ass in here chillin' under the AC and shit."

"That show was really nice," Queen mentioned. "I told you how he keeps me wet just thinking about him. His swag and style, I can over-dose from him, girl,"

"Girl, you know he wants to hit that ass!"

"I know, I know. I just don't know. All I can do is pray like always. I can't keep doing this," Queen told Cookie.

"I hear you. You're my girl, you know we roll together. I'm going shopping later if you wit' it."

"That's the last thing on my mind,"

"Okay, just checkin',"

"I will get at you later,"

Cookie gave Queen a hug and left.

* * *

Ring, Ring,

"Yo', what's good, Ta'Rod," Kaleem spoke as he answered his phone.

"I heard that last week a bum killed Black and two of his workers."

"What? Are you sure?" Kaleem asked.

"Man, stop askin' stupid fuckin' questions, hell yeah I'm sure. We gave Hass five stacks!"

"Pump your breaks, take it fuckin' easy. I told you that Hass don't bullshit and handle his business. He not gonna take from me. How could a bum get that close to Black? Shit don't sound right. I'll hit you back! Let me text Hass now." Kaleem said and then hung up.

"What's good Haas, you get that job done?"

"Yeah, just bring my package to me, my nigga,"

"Give me about two hours, I got ya',"

"Ok, I'll be waitin'."

Kaleem stopped on Avon to grab the dough from Ish.

"What's good bro? Everything good, here is four stacks and put me an order in for a whole one."

"I will have it brought to ya'. Be easy." Kaleem stated, left, and then dialed Hass.

"What up?" Hass answered.

"I'm on my way to ya'," Kaleem told him and then hung up.

"What's the business, Kaleem?"

"Yeah, Haas, niggas talkin' about a bum/crack head, killed Black and shot two of his workers,"

"Call me what you want. I took care of it as I said I would. Black got three bullets; the workers got one apiece in the back. Let's just say they call me Hawk, sometimes,"

"Here is yo' cash that's six altogether," Kaleem told him.

"Now that's why I fuck with you," Haas replied. "Yo', Kaleem, by the way, you ever heard of a body blast?"

"Nah, what's that?"

"You don't want to know," Haas smirked.

Kaleem shook his head, "Later."

When he left, he called Ta'Rod. "Yo', Ta'Rod... That was our man. Like I told you, he is good at what he do," Kaleem said.

"You sure?"

"Don't ask no stupid fuckin' question," Kaleem replied just like Ta'Rod told him earlier.

CHAPTER 18

"What's up, Ta'Rod?" Kaleem said.

"The spot on Thirteenth St. got robbed last night and Kim was killed."

"What! Who the fuck did it?"

"We got to make sure, but looks like members of the Young Mafia Gang. She wouldn't give them the combo to her safe. You know they couldn't carry it. Word is it was three of them." Ta'Rod stated.

"This some bullshit, joker, don't want you to eat at all. We just took that lost with Black."

"It's hot over there right now. Sooner or later our names gonna start jumpin'. You know the city is covered with Young Mafia's Gang," Ta'Rod said.

"I don't care they ain't handling us like that. I don't care how big their organization is, they gone have to bury me like they did Kim before I let them get away with that shit," Kaleem pressed.

* * *

Kim was a straight ride or die chick, gangsta. It's been three weeks since Kim's murder. Little Eddie was a five-foot tall beast! He carried a stainless steel Smith & Wesson forty-four with an eight-inch barrel and six-inch titan scope. No one could ever suspect how insane he was. He always looked for a way to repay his lifelong friend, Kaleem. Kaleem never turned his back on Lil Eddie. Lil Eddie could remember clearly that Saturday morning when they both were crossing Central Avenue and Eighth Street going to get their haircut when a stolen Acura Legend was speeding and lost control. It jumped the sidewalk. It seemed like Lil Eddie sneakers were glued to the sidewalk until Kaleem grab his arm and pulled him out of the way, as they watched the Legend crash into the brick wall of the apartment building. *The sight of the driver's head stuck in the windshield was crazy.* Both teenagers were killed. Lil Eddie always focused on repaying his debt. He knew that the Young Mafia Gang had murdered Kim.

Kim's sister Amani takes care of her two kids now, Khayyirrah and Kareemah. Kaleem and Ta'Rod made sure all the expenses were paid in full; it was a small private setting. Kim was a straight ride or die chick, gangsta. Kaleem found one family foreclosed house that Saleem was about to let go so he gave it to Amani. That's small to the respect Kim earned from him.

While downtown Newark, Lil Eddie saw the lieutenant of the Young Mafia, Tony, walking with his girlfriend shopping. It was three o'clock in the afternoon and packed as always.

Lil Eddie hits Fat Mike. "Yo, this Lil Eddie," he stated when Fat Mike answered.

"What's good homie?"

"Fat Mike, I got an emergency at hand,"

"Go head holla',"

"I'm downtown and about to handle some business and need a getaway car, something fast in the next half-hour,"

"I'm on Prince Street now; I will hit you in twenty,"

"That's what it is." the phones hung up.

Lil Eddie was persistent on killing Tony today. Tony went into the Chinese Store to buy some jewelry. Lil Eddie brought a dread wig from the wig store next door. There was no way Tony was getting away.

Lil Eddie phone began to vibrate. "What's up?"

"I'm five minutes away; I got a black mustang with a half tank from Society Hills,"

"Okay, park it on Bradford Place on the left side of the street. You know, Terry, with the hot dog stand."

"Yeah, yeah," Fat Mike replied.

"I'ma give him my car keys, get them and I will get my car from you later,"

"That's what it do." They hung up.

Tony and his chick were in Dr. Jays, perfect timing. "Terry, what's up?"

"Chillin'."

"I need you to give my keys to Fat Mike, he should come by in about ten minutes. You got, it?"

"No problem,"

"Thanks, my man."

Lil Eddie slides the wig and shades on and was ready for action! Lil Eddie knew there was a Newark cop on the first floor of Dr. Jays, so he knew he had to get super close to Tony. Good! Tony and his girl walked to the second floor of the store. Tony sat down while the girl grabbed two pairs of Baby Phat jeans that were on sale for one hundred and eighty dollars apiece.

Lil Eddie grabbed four pairs of Pepe jeans, pulled out his 007 knife and opened it; putting it in his right hand under the jeans. *"Damn,"* he thought he saw the girl come out the dressing room.

"Tony, how do these make my ass look?"

"Baby, get you two pairs of them," he replied. She turned to walk back to change again.

"Yo', let me sit these here," Lil Eddie said.

When Tony looked up, he tried to grab Lil Eddie's arm, but it was too late, the blade penetrated Tony's neck into his jugular vein! Tony's girl came out screaming as she saw the blood pumping from his neck like a fire hydrant. Employees and the police officers were running up the stairs as Lil Eddie was walking down the stairs. The officer called for a paramedic and back up. He then removed the nine-millimeter Tony had in his waistband, giving it to the crime scene unit when they arrived. Lil Eddie jumped in the stolen Mustang as planned and peeled off! Nobody knew who stabbed Tony. The ambulance rushed Tony to University Medical where he was pronounced DOA (Dead On Arrival.) This meant an all-out war, but with who? Kaleem or Ta'Rod didn't have any idea who did Tony in. The question was, were they ready for war?

* * *

"Damn, Green, it's been two months since that guy Rick's murder, and we ain't got anywhere,"

"He was messing with those little girls and he got what he dissevered you ask me," said Murray.

"Well, he can't do it anymore that's for damn sure," Green responded. "Murray you want to grab a few drinks?"

"I'ma have to take a rain check on that. I told the wifey I would be in early tonight,"

"I understand that,"

"I heard over the radio, some guy got stabbed up downtown while shopping,"

"Man, it's so many young kids that are hurting, lost and mislead on those streets. They do just what the system was made for them to do and that is to kill themselves off," Green stated.

"I got to go, later."

"Later," Green replied and walked off.

Murray stopped Mark in the hallway. "Hey Mark, I was just talking to Green about how these young guys don't have any positive role models out to show them how to be men. That's why the graveyards, Trenton, Rahway, Bordentown, Yardville and the rest are full."

Things were jumping crazy, back-to-back. Shit was stinking all over town. The streets were talking even before they pronounced Tony dead at the trauma unit at University. Everyone wanted to know who caught Tony slipping like that.

* * *

"Whoever it was is a monster! You know you got beef when you have to keep your hand on your heat! More money, more problems, what's up?" Mr. Devil said to Kaleem as he was driving.

"Not right now," Kaleem thought. *"Damn homie it's like that? You're the devil!"*

"You got that right. We know who I am now you got to let the streets know who you are."

"Yeah, yeah, you right!"

"I know I'm right. It's time for war, guns poppin' and bodies droppin'," the Devil said. *"I'ma roll with ya', son. They hattin' on you hard feel me,"*

That shit had Kaleem paranoid. The Devil was in his head once again. He grabbed a spot located in Flanders, New Jersey, about an hour from Newark— beautiful, about a hundred apartments sitting on a hill. People spoke and kept it moving.

Driving from Flanders, he took route 206 to route 80 to 280, jumped on the Garden State Parkway and got off in Irvington to holler at Ta'Rod over on 21st Street and Hopkins.

"What's up with ya' man?" Kaleem asked.

"We got to put a stop to Robo Cop," Ta'Rod said with Kaleem agreeing.

CHAPTER 19

Tony's funeral is today at Perry's. The place was packed as two black hearses pulled into the parking lot. Because it was two other services going on, cars were lined up doubled-parked on Springfield Ave., Court St., Lincoln, and on High St. It was a gloomy day. The temperature was 50 degrees with a chance of rain. It was a sad day.

The inside was full; standing room only, people were standing wall-to-wall. Four Columbians were pushing both caskets into the funeral home. Tony's funeral service began: "Ladies and gentlemen, my name is Pastor Love. We come here today to lay to rest a twenty-seven-year-old young man. His life was cut short due to the gang violence that has been destroying our community."

"Amen," said a few people.

"Yes, yes, yes," said another woman.

"The Lord giveth and the Lord taketh away," Pastor Love continued, "We must plan for something, or we will fall for anything. It is a sad thing how we have turned against each other. Our ancestors fought for segregation and against slavery for us to have better lives today and this is not the way we thank them!" You could hear a pin drop in that place. Pastor Love went on to say, "Look at how many fatherless households there are. How many kids grow up without their father? I want all the guys in here to ask yourself this… Do my actions in life show I am a man? Do I carry morals, values, responsibility, and respect? A man is not measured in his valuable but in what he values!"

Some of the guys in the crowd knew he was talking to them. The others could have punched the pastor in his mouth. "That's right!" a few baby mamas' said.

Pastor, continued, "God made you guys Kings, Leaders, Fathers, Providers, Husbands, Uncles, and Friends. Too many times we're caught up in our own selfish motives, then we are quick to say the white man this, the white man that, but what are you doing for the black man?"

The Columbians rolled the caskets to the front, behind the Pastor. Women were crying and the thugs were teary-eyed.

"Ladies and gentlemen, please join me in prayer," said the Pastor. "Father God, please be with Tony as he comes to you. Let us take this time to get our life in…"

Tat, Tat, Tat, Tat, Tat, Tat, Bullets was spraying the place. Four Columbians began firing back.

"It's a hit!" someone from Young Mafia yelled out as they returned fire…

Boom, Boom, Pop, Pop, Tat, Tat,

One of the Columbians fell backward as he took a bullet in the middle of his forehead. The Columbians dressed in all black were not playing any games. They were talking with their hands and eyes only. One picked up his partners' Mac-11 and continued to fire on Big Jay and his crew. The Columbians positioned themselves with one leading the way with the other two walking backward still firing at everyone. Once outside, a black Benz pulled up with a smoke black tint. It stayed in the middle of Mercer St. right before the corner of Lincoln St. Just before the last Columbian got into the car he pulled out a remote and pressed the button... Boom! Boom! Two cars exploded in the funeral home's parking lot. Boom, Boom, was the sound of the blast, from two more cars that became inflamed by fire, smoke, and metal flying all over the place.

The three men jumped into the car and were gone. Sirens were screaming, the bombs were so powerful they even flipped over a few cars near them. Blood and dead bodies were all over the place, with bullet holes everywhere. People were crying and running not knowing what to do. Big Jay saw his right-hand man Greg had been hit. So he dragged him to his Range Rover pushed cars out the way and drove on the sidewalk to get out the area before the cops came.

The police were all over the place. Newark Police Department was in full gear. "World War III!" one officer said.

"I never saw anything like this," said another.

"This is a catastrophe!" Detective Kojack replied.

"It's gonna be a long day. Better get ready," said Green.

It was taped off from Broome St. all the way to High St. "Don't let no other cars leave!"

* * *

Big Jay turned into the hospital. "I got you, homie, I got you, homie." Greg didn't reply! Big Jay looked and saw Greg's eyes were closed. "Don't leave me, nigga, open your fuckin' eyes, open ya' eyes!" He laid Greg on the sidewalk of the hospital entrance and peeled off in his

Range Rover. With murder on his mind, Big Jay was furious! He called for a meeting on Seymour Avenue ASAP! Within an hour, the apartment was packed.

The meeting began. "We lost a lot of homies today. I want whoever is behind this shit I want them dead, their mother and kids too! Put out a ten thousand dollar reward out for anyone with some solid information and proof on who done it. I want them before the cops do. Greg did not make it. He lost too much blood by the time I got him to the hospital. So you mean to tell me, nobody seen shit!" Big Jay stated.

"Shit happened so fast," L Murder said.

"Who had security in the parking lot?" Animal said to L Murder.

"Paco, I saw you flat line that one guy. You were making your gun sing, son! That's what I expected all my team to do." Big Jay said and continued, "All the people there should have been bustin' their guns!"

"They weren't amateurs," L Murder stated.

"Murder, you, and Animal come up front. You stand right there," Bac! Was the sound of Big Jay's gun putting a hole in Animals brain, pushing a spray of blood over L Murders face and shirt, Animal's lifeless body fell to the floor. "That's for him not comin' in bustin' his gun!"

"Aight, anybody else can't bust their gun? Head shots only," said Paco.

"We with ya' big homie," another replied.

"Five poppin', jokers droppin'!" yelled Vedo.

"I want y'all to comb 'Brick City' like a tsunami." Some members were mesmerized by the way; Big Jay blew Animals brain out in the meeting.

Zell helped bodyguard the body. "The popo's gonna be all over this so watch ya' ass."

"On my dead momma, if that bitch as nigga, Kaleem is involved, toe tag his ass. Matter of fact, I wanna do him myself." Big Jay was angry and everyone knew not to say the wrong thing. They all reloaded and hit the streets of 'Brick City'. No way was Young Mafia going out like that.

* * *

"What's the business?" Ta'Rod asked Kaleem.

"Slow motion ain't shit,"

"Man, O' girl from the hospital got your head fucked up. You still didn't cut yet?"

"Nah,"

"What the fuck, you really loosin' it,"

"Man, she got me fucked up," Kaleem agreed.

"You better get a grip. Next thing you know, you will be wanting to get married. Now that's what I call a tender dick ass joker,"

* * *

"Did anybody notify the director, Mr. Baye?"

"No, not yet," said Kojack.

Whitehead and Kojack analyzed the inside of the funeral home. "This is something, bodies everywhere. I need to retire after this year, Kojack I can't take this much longer. It is sad for the families and victims."

"I agree," Whitehead, answered.

"There go, Detective Murray,"

"What's good guys? It looks bad around here. How many bodies we're talking?" Murray asked.

"Hold on, here comes the Coroner now,"

"We got twenty-five dead fellas; twelve wounded twenty others with broken bones, cuts and springs, minor stuff like that," said the Coroner.

"Okay, make sure I get a printout on everything you got," said Murray.

Robo Cop walked on the set. "Damn, what a mess we got here," he said. "I want to say it is a gang war, but who would be crazy enough to go against Big Jay. Man, if they want to shoot and kill each other, let them do what they want. They destroy where they live and secure my job,"

"You're a big asshole Robo," Murray said. "For the record, many of us on the force live in these same neighborhoods. We have family members here as well. So when a fucking jerk like you, that live an hour or two away, that just care about money, ain't shit!"

"So hold on," said Robo Cop.

"You better take a walk Robo," said Green.

"Check this out, Murray," Green replied, "the disturbing effects of violence should make us all reflect on ourselves, our ethics, and beliefs. Violence hurts us all. You will run into people that don't care about people and most of them don't care about themselves. I pray every night that our people realize that the fight is not against each other. It is excruciatingly painful, frustrating, and depressing. On top of that, the economic dilemma that hurts us every day." Murray saw the water that formed inside Green's eyes, so he knew he spoke from the heart.

"Let's go do these reports, did you know Internal Affairs are looking into all the complaints that Robo Cop has been shaking down dealers. So he has his plate full if that shit is true," Green said.

"Let's get out of here." they both agreed and left.

CHAPTER 20

"Money over hoe's, we all we got," stated Ta'Rod.

"We all we got," Kaleem repeated.

"With all the heat from the funeral home, murders had everywhere hot. If Perry's Funeral home wasn't on the map it was now! It's been weeks and it was still on the news."

"I know, Ta'Rod, the Feds might get on that. I'm glad we ain't in the shit. Whoever it was don't play no games. Yo' we need to lock the Academy Spyers Projects down on buyin' our product,"

"I got Kenny's number with the Maroon Honda Accord that rolls with Bam with the beauty parlor on Clinton Avenue, with all those fine girls workin' for him. I will hit him up later,"

"I want that cash flow over there; make him an offer he can't refuse,"

"I'm on it, I told you. I'm gonna hit the New Jersey Pac tonight,"

"We better lay low a little longer,"

"C'mon, man, we gucci!"

"I'ma chill," Kaleem told him,"

"Aight, I'ma bounce, peace."

* * *

Newark Homicide Squad and Newark Sheriff Department teamed up to find the underlying cause of the Perry Funeral Home murders. At the Sheriff Department, Director Mr. Baye began the meeting. "Good afternoon, people. Word on the streets is that the funeral home killings stem from the murder of Kim Brown on Thirteenth Street. Kaleem Ward is said to be running that spot, so pick him up for questioning, he is driving an all-black Honda Accord plate number RH1 Jersey tags. His partner, Ta'Rod Andrews, drives a blue Caprice plate number DJ-Man Jersey tags also. Pick up Jamal in Lil Bricks his crew is said to have beef with Big Jay and his Young Mafia Gang, also, Lopez on Broadway in North Newark in the Broadway townhouses. I want to send a message that we are on their asses and it will damn sure slow down their money flow. These people are armed and dangerous, so proceed with extreme caution. See what you can find out. We have the Mayor, City Council, and the public on our ass. Elections are coming up and we don't need any more heat. Right now, I'ma turn the floor to Detective Greene…

"Good Afternoon ladies and gentlemen; I have E-mailed all of you the name and addresses of these guys. Again, as Mr. Baye stated they are considered dangerous! If you guys get any leads let us know right away. We can only hold them for seventy-two hours without charging them. Most of them know that. So question them and get them out of here. We don't need a lawsuit on top of this shit. That's all I have for you."

"Mr. Baye, we will help Mayor Booker live up to his promise of making crime a top priority. I also want Big Jay and his Young Mafia Gang shook up also. It's going to be a war if they find out before we do."

Director Baye continued, "The Benz was stolen out of Long Island a week before on Hempstead Avenue. We found no prints in the car. They dumped the car on Hanes Avenue by the Newark Airport and got into a backup car. The dead Columbian is Michael Goichberg. We got a dead Columbian with two forty-caliber bullets in his forehead. What I'm saying right now is we don't have shit! The Mayor tells me we have a news conference this week. Okay, guys be safe out there." he stated waved a hand and left out.

* * *

"Yo', Ta'Rod, they picked up Lopez from North Newark last night or the day before,"

"They gonna be looking for our asses too," said Ta'Rod.

"That Italian lawyer from Hoboken, Mr. De Valle I'ma retain him."

"How much?" Ta'Rod asked.

"Twenty stacks, he is one of the best. He won't be back in town until, November 10th."

"Damn," Ta'Rod said.

"Stay low,"

"That's what it is, fam,"

"Later, Ta'Rod,"

"Aight, later, Kaleem."

"Damn, I'm slippin'. I forgot to give Ta'Rod one of the Blackberries Santos sent. " Kaleem said to himself after he already left Ta'Rod. He picked up his phone and called

Ta'Rod. "Yo', Ta'Rod I got a phone for you from Santos. It's only for incoming calls, so don't give the number to *no* one,"

"I got ya'. Leave it at the spot, and I'll pick it up,"

"Okay, later," Kaleem replied.

* * *

Robo Cop was putting pressure on many drug dealers in Newark. He also been putting more and more cocaine up his nose as well; staying up for days at a time. His wife Robin knew something was wrong, but was afraid to confront him. It was to the point she was threatening to leave if he didn't straighten up.

"Honey, we need to talk," Robin told Robo Cop.

"Talk about what?" he replied.

"About us, the kids, our family, for Christ sakes, Roy!"

"Damn Robin, I bust my ass working, putting my life on the line and all you want to do is bitch and moan,"

"But honey…"

"But honey, nothing," he cut her off. "We will talk about this another time. I got to go," he said, walking out the door, slamming it.

Anger and rage were still on his mind as he reached Newark. He drove to Fifteenth Ave, and Fairmont Ave. He spotted Shaheed complete a sale.

He quickly got out the car. "Don't you run; hands behind yo' back!"

"For what?"

"'Cause I'ma bust your head open if you don't, that's why!" He handcuffed Shaheed to a pole. He walked to the garbage can and pulled out two packs of coke vials, two fifty altogether. *"This what I'm talkin' about,"* Robo Cop thought to himself, with thoughts of keeping it.

"That ain't my shit!" Shaheed spat.

"Let me search ya' ass! How much is this, Mr. Shaheed, this is a lot of money,"

"It's a thousand dollars, that's it,"

"I'ma help you out, I don't feel like doing any paperwork. I'ma take this down to the station and say the suspect dropped this while he was running away from me."

Shaheed had the look of a killer. "Do what the hell you want. You got the upper hand now."

"Tell your big homie, payroll starts next week, to make sure I'm on it. Now beat it!" he told him after removing the handcuffs.

* * *

A patrol car radios, "This is car 134 we see the suspect Jamal going into a store on Bergen and Avon. Bring him in or wait for backup?" a patrol car radioed.

"Ten four, car 134 bring him into Green St. Approach with caution, over?"

"That's a ten-four out!"

The officer that radioed in approached Jamal with caution as told. "Jamal today isn't your lucky day. You're under arrest!"

"For what?" Jamal inquired.

"Just take it easy. You will find out when you get downtown," the officer told him.

"This some bullshit,"

"He got anything on him, partner?"

"No, he is clean."

When the patrol car pulled to the gate on Green St, Jamal thought, *"Why they didn't take me to the Fourth Prescient on 17th Avenue."*

"This is car 134 we got one for homicide squad…"

"A Homicide!" Jamal screamed, "What the hell is going on?" he said.

The officers took Jamal inside the building and sat him down, still handcuffed.

"Jamal, I'm Kevin from the Sheriff department. You done fucked up now. We know you called the hit on Big Jay and his crew. We know y'all were beefing. You are going down forever! Billy, down in Trenton State Prison waiting to beat ya' ass,"

Jamal sat speechless,

"Jamal, I'm Detective Greene and I want to help you out this mess. I know you don't want to go down for this,"

"No. I don't know shit,"

"Hold on, hear me out, if you help us, we can help you."

"Like I said we got yo' ass," Kevin said.

"Well, like I said, I don't know shit,"

"I hope you got some pussy last night because you're gonna be somebody's girl in prison."

"Ain't no gay shit here, promise that. As far as getting pussy last night, I bust about four nuts. Two were in ya' wife's mouth and the other two in her ass!"

Slap! Kevin slapped Jamal out of the chair. Detective Greene rushed up and grabbed Kevin.

"You hit like a bitch! I see why she wants new dick," Jamal told him, making him angrier.

"What the hell is going on in here?" asked Mr. Baye. "He knows anything?"

"He ain't talking," Kevin answered.

"Obviously, he ain't! Get him out of here," Mr. Baye responded.

"We will be seeing you, Jamal," Kevin told him, giving him a look letting him know he wasn't playing.

"Fuck you," Jamal spat not letting the look intimidate him. *"His punk ass better not get caught slippin."* Jamal thought.

* * *

"I hope this some good stuff." Robo Cop said to himself as he emptied eight vials of coke onto his twenty-dollar bill. He pushed his nose into the bill almost losing his breath. *"Yeah, this is some fucking good stuff."* He wiped the residue from his nose. *"I got to get to that Kaleem, he gonna make me fucking rich."* Robo Cop said to himself aloud. "If I would have known about the spots in New Hope and Georgia King Village, I would have got some of that money as well."

* * *

After they released Jamal, he called his homie. "Yo', Jonny B, get the word out popo pickin' up niggas for that shit at the funeral home. I just left Greene St. I'ma grab us some phones to be on the safe side.

"That's the business," Johnny B responded.

"Six." replied Jamal.

"Six."

* * *

Lopez didn't tell the police anything either. His lawyer called and told them he is in California and will be back in town tomorrow morning.

"Lopez, here is my card if you can help us," said Mr. Baye.

"I don't need that shit. I was born not to snitch! That's your job that you get paid to do, not mine," said Lopez.

"Don't get caught slipping with all the dope you pushing," Kevin told him.

"It is what it is, homes!"

Lopez girlfriend was in front waiting for him in his gray 850 BMW Coupe. CoCo was a beautiful pecan complexion Latino knockout. Lopez stepped out and smiled as he jumped in his car.

"We got to get to the bottom of this," said Mr. Baye.

"Just a matter of when. Let's go across the street to Spain's Restaurant to grab something to eat," Greene said.

"Sounds like a winner." Mr. Baye agreed.

* * *

Zzzz, Zzzz,

Kaleem's Blackberry started vibrating. "Yo', what up, boss?" he said as he answered the phone.

"Qué pasa, my friend?" Santos responded. "My friend, I seen in your eyes when we first met that it was going to be good business between you and me. You have been doing very well. I see you ran into a little trouble. Just know you are never alone, I am always around."

"I got ya', boss, I respect that."

"There are two kinds of people in this world: those in your corner and those that are not. When you surround yourself with toxic people they will suck you dry," Santos stated.

"It's a little hot over here right now. We doing big numbers in B-More, Cherry Hill, and South Carolina. I estimate three hundred a month with just them."

"Kaleem, you play poker, no?"

"Yeah, I play, boss."

"Well, in this game you got to have a purpose and know when to fold ya' hand,"

"Boss, I'ma keep that in mind, like I said, loyalty carry you a long way in life."

"I got you covered my words are action, good night."

"Yeah, of course, boss." They disconnected the call.

Santos already knew it was hot over there. Kaleem recognized that nothing lasts forever. Right now, Kaleem was eating, money wasn't a thang. The clientele was crazy. *"I love 'Brick City',"* Kaleem thought after he got off the phone.

CHAPTER 21

Ring, Ring,

"How was your day, Queen?" Kaleem asked when Queen answered.

"Fine how are you?"

"I'm good. As always you have been on my mind today,"

"I had a long day at work and now getting ready for church in the morning. As a matter of fact, why don't you come with me, Kaleem?"

"Damn, church." he thought. "Sure," he told her, thinking, *"This will give me a chance to be around her."*

"Good, well meet me at the Dunkin' Donuts by where the Haze Home Project was,"

"On Springfield by the Post Office, I know all about Newark," he replied.

"I'll meet you there at 10:30 sharp. Don't be late," she added.

"If I can come spend the night with you I won't be late."

"That's cute, but I trust you to be on time. Good night, Mr. Kaleem."

"Good night, Queen."

Church, Kaleem hadn't been to church since he was a kid. Lightning will hit him soon as he walks through them doors.

"Do I really want to go?" was a question that he asked himself.

"Man, listen to me," the Devil told him. *"You need to go fuck something, we ain't get any since yo' ass been chasing that nurse. On top of that, she ain't doing nothing."*

"She's not like the others; only want what they can get," Kaleem thought.

"What's wrong with that?"

"What's wrong with it is, everybody and their daddies done been up in 'em! Ain't no secrets to them at all. I don't want to hear this shit, I'm going to sleep."

"I'll be here when you wake up," he told him devilishly.

* * *

Sunday Morning.

Kaleem got to Dunkin Donuts at ten O'clock. There was no way he was going to be late.

"Good morning, Mr. Kaleem, I see you made it," Queen told him when she pulled up.

"Your presence is medication to my soul when I am around you, baby,"

"Stop, not on Sunday, Kaleem!"

"I'm in tune with my heart every day of the week. What church are we going to?" he inquired.

"It's St. Elizabeth on Chancellor Avenue. Everyone is family, Faye was there last month, and she knows she was blessed to sing."

"That's fine, I'll follow you."

They pulled their cars around the side of the church in the parking lot. *"This is perfect."* Kaleem thought referring to the parking lot because he didn't want his car parked on the main avenue.

"Hello, my name is Dorothy. Greetings in the name of the Lord, welcome to Saint Elizabeth," greeted the usher as they walked up. "Good morning, Queen, you are such a beautiful person. I pray you and your guest have a good time in the house of the Lord today,"

"Why thank you, Dorothy, as always, filled with the glow of the Lord,"

"Please go on in, service is about to start. Right, this way please." They walked through the doors of the church and sat where directed.

"Listen up," Pastor Nadir said to the crowd. He was a sharp looking man, brown-skinned with a low haircut.

"I wonder is he a Reverend Ike too." Kaleem sarcastically thought.

"Ain't God good?" he asked.

"All the time," the crowded church replied.

"Some people dressed to kill. Some dress normally. But everyone seems to be happy, both young and old people." Nadir continued. "I want you all to know that God loves you, no matter what you may have done or who you are. I want to know why we only call God when we got problems. I'm not going to preach today, I want to teach! I will give pragmatic solutions to everyday problems, using scripture as my format and guide. The foundation every religion should stand on is love; it is our job to love each other. Deacon, please if you would bring me two bags from inside the vacuum cleaners and a pitcher of water please, sir. While he is grabbing those things, allow me to share this. I went to the mall shopping last week and while I was parking my truck, I saw these two women yelling and screaming at each other. One said, 'you are stupid as hell, you saw me waiting on this parking spot!' the other replied, 'I graduated from Princeton University.' and Princeton is a great school, but while they were still debating, another car had taken the parking space they were fighting to get." The congregation laughed. This man had a way to keep your attention.

"He is real good," said Queen.

The Deacon returned with the items the Pastor had requested. The Pastor then took the pitcher of water and poured it over the top of his head, drenched his whole body. He opened up the bag from the vacuum cleaners, ripped it open, and shook the dirt from his head to his feet. The church was silent.

"This joker is crazy," Kaleem said as he looked over at Queen.

Mr. Devil began to speak again. *"Man, I told you this place is crazy. I can't stand places like this, we don't get along."*

"I guess not," Kaleem thought.

"You know how I get down. I will give you what you need. We partners to the end, feel me,"

"To the end of what?"

"You want to get this money or what?" the Devil pressed.

"Man you bugging, I'ma holla' at you later."

The church was beautiful, big colorful stained windows, laced with wall-to-wall red carpet. The benches had a thick red comfortable cushion to sit on. There were so many women and very few men.

Queens's eyes were glued to the Pastor as he began to speak. "I know you all think I've lost my mind up here,"

"I damn sure do." Kaleem thought.

"No, I just want you to know I am no better than any of you sitting out there! We all have sinned, and fell short– we all are sinners. Amen! Now I am about to teach. Whenever I speak, I speak for myself as well. People, too many of us measure people by their valuables. Our valuables do not make us who we are! Amen!"

"Hallelujah, say it again, preacher!" someone from the crowd yelled.

"I said you are worth more than your valuables! 'Cause if they are taken from you, then who are you?" he asked. "I mean the gossip is terrible. So and so son went to jail last week, well did you ask if you could help with anything. Huh? Don't get quiet on me now! Amen!"

"Go head Pastor!" another person from the crowd said.

"We are all God's children, right? Many of us must change our cognition that we are all God's children. When you see drug dealers or users on the street, what is the first thing you hear? 'Look at them selling that stuff or look at them using that stuff.' How many of us have ever taken the time to speak to them or let them know they are loved. Many of them are hurting and in pain. I'm on fire now, somebody better tell me to stop!"

"More Pastor, go head!" a member told him, fanning a hand in the air.

"You have to read a book before you judge it. God always knows what he is doing," he continued. "I know a man that killed someone that was beating his mother with a baseball bat. The kid was sixteen when it happened. He received a life sentence. After fifteen years of the judicial system, his sentence got overturned! Now he is in society saying he changed his life. Now it's not our job to judge him at all. I want you to turn your Bibles to Psalms 107 verses 6-7. 'Then they cried unto the Lord in their trouble, and he delivered them from out of their distress. And he led them forth by the right way, that they might go to a city of habitation.' Look at verse 10, 'Some sat in darkness, in utter darkness, prisoners suffering in iron chains,' Then in verse 16, he says, 'for he breaks down gates of bronze and cuts through bars of iron.' Now my question is, how many of us are still in prison, even though, you can do and go as you like every day? Let us go to the Throne of the Lord in prayer. God, we thank you for this day, and all you do, touch the sick and needy, the many men and women in prisons across America. Look over our government also. Forgive us of our many sins. I am living for you now God and thank you for forgiving a murderer like me."

"The Pastor even busts his guns," said the devil.

"Damn," Kaleem thought. That blew him away.

"In the name of Jesus, we ask for your blessings. Amen!" Pastor Nadir ended.

"Amen... Amen... Amen..." sounded off the church.

Kaleem felt every word the Pastor said. He was waiting and wanted to be forgiven. The choir began to sing. The people were clapping their hands and dancing to the Lord. Now that was the joy and happiness that just can't be bought or sold.

"I hope you enjoyed yourself," Queen asked Kaleem after service was over.

"This was surely an experience I will always recall. Thank you for inviting me, Queen. I mean, that Pastor is the truth! I can relate to him. He turned it out,"

"That's how he gets down. He rolled in the streets of Newark. Well, in the Central and South Wards,"

"He don't hold any punches back, he tells it like it is. He is real,"

"Hi, Queen," Malika and Peewee spoke as they walked up.

"Hi, girls, what's up? "

"Nothing much just came over to say hello to you and your guest," said Malika.

"This is Kaleem. Kaleem this is Malika and Peewee they are friends of mine."

"Please to meet you both," he replied.

"You lucky you're my girl, Queen," Malika said as she walked off.

"Don't mind her," Peewee whispered. "Talk to you later, Queen. Take it easy. Nice meeting you as well, Kaleem."

"Okay, call me later, Peewee," Queen told her, putting her attention back to Kaleem. "I usually go to my mom's house to eat breakfast when she doesn't go to church. You are welcome to come if you like,"

"I don't eat pork."

"We don't either, Mr."

"There is not a need to drive both cars, I can drive, and then bring you to pick up yours later," Kaleem said.

"Sure. That would be fine,"

All eyes were on them as they jumped into the Accord.

"Man, what a relief!" Queen said as she got into the car.

"What makes you say that?"

"Because everybody and their momma gonna want to know who you are."

"Just tell them yo' husband," Kaleem stated jokingly. However, deep inside, he was very serious.

"Yeah right, you want them to really talk,"

As they drove downtown Newark, it was many people out walking around and shopping.

"Maybe we can check out the PAC (New Jersey Preforming Arts Center) soon," Kaleem said. "I have been meaning to ask you, what kind of perfume is that, Queen?"

"DOLCE & GABBANA,"

"It smells nice."

"Thank you, Kaleem. I see you remember how to get to her house,"

"Of course, I recall anything important, baby,"

"I bet you do,"

Kaleem looked over at Queen when he stopped at the light and said, "Queen, actually I really want to understand your philosophy. I want the chance to enter your world."

"Right now I don't have time for a man, Kaleem," she said blowing him off again.

"I'm spellbound, never have I wanted anyone like I want you. Not being conceited, I never had no problem getting a woman. I know it is something that connects me to you."

"The light changed, Kaleem," she said pointing forward.

"My bad." he turned right and found a park in front of her mother's apartment. "You grew up in Jersey City?"

"Yes, on Park Street. I also lived on Clerk Street and Myrtle Avenue. Then I got the job in Newark at the hospital,"

"You are such a complete woman,"

"Stop making me blush, Kaleem,"

"Your mom's ever thought about moving?"

"No, she says all her friends are over here. I check on her often and try to stay on top of her health. Plus now she has Alzheimer as well,"

"She seems to be on point to me,"

"Come on, let's go inside." Queen insisted.

* * *

Knock, Knock,

"Who is it?" Inez asked.

"It's your favorite daughter!"

"I guess 'cause you're my only daughter. Hi Sweetie," she responded as she was opening the door.

"Hi, Ma,"

"Hello, Ms. Inez,"

"Hi, son, how are you?"

"I'm good,"

"How are you Ma?"

"I'm to bless to be stressed; I stayed up late last night watching the BET's celebration of the Gospel. It was so good, girl. I cooked some turkey bacon, grits, raising bread and eggs. I hope that's enough?"

"That's a lot Ma,"

"Anything for my baby, and you too, Kaleem,"

"Why thank you, Ms. Inez."

"Whatever God does is for the best." as she always says.

"Church was really great, Ma. Pastor Nadir really allowed God to use him today. I enjoy hearing him preach,"

"That's good to have found a church that's still based on one thing and that's spreading the good news of the gospel. People seem to forget that they are sinners and we all belong to God," Inez continued. "You two go ahead and eat, I have things to do in the room."

"Do you have a big appetite Kaleem," Queen asked.

"It depends on how you feed me, baby,"

"You know what I mean, Kaleem," Queen smiled.

"Just a regular plate will be fine,"

"Would you like milk or orange juice?"

"Orange juice is fine,"

"Not a problem, Mr. Kaleem."

"I hope your moms can cook," he stated playfully.

"You better not talk about my mom's cooking,"

"I'm just saying," he said with a smile.

"If you don't want her to give you the beat down,"

"Nah, baby, it is good."

"It is a shame that I had to scare you to say that," Queen said and they both laughed.

"Kaleem, I want to ask you a question," Queen asked.

"Sure,"

"What do you know about HIV and AIDS?"

"I know it's a drop in a person's immune function. That it can't fight off the virus. It comes from gay men, people sharing needles, or having unprotected sex. What makes you ask?"

"Because I want to be totally fair with you, I have feelings for you and I have to stop seeing you. I have AIDS,"

"What!" Kaleem yelled in a hurt and angry tone caught off guard with her reply. "Why the fuck you ain't tell me you have that shit! You been playing games with me. This some straight bullshit,"

Tears rolled down Queens' face. She tried to hold herself together, knowing her mother was still in the next room. "Kaleem, I have only dated and had sex with two people in my lifetime; I have been having it for fifteen years. I tried to find out which one gave it to me, but both say they don't have it, and neither wants to go get tested."

"I can't believe this bullshit," he responded, still shocked at what he just heard. I wanted to be a part of your life and you wasted all this time before you told me this shit."

"People don't see you as human when they find out a person have AIDS. I blame God for this! I don't know when I'm going to die. I don't deserve this! I refuse to give this to anyone, never in a million years. I spend a lot of time reading about what will eventually end my life. The Aaron Diamond AIDS Research Center has a bunch of scientists that are trying to fight this battle as well. See the doctors don't know exactly what cells could protect the body from the infection. The reality is HIV and AIDS remain a deadly epidemic in America."

"Damn, why me." Kaleem thought.

"I panicked at first as well. I'm sorry, Kaleem. I pray that you understand. I realize that God loves me no matter what. My self-love, morals, and values help me through the day. With God's love and my mother, I learned that 'Whatever God does is for the best,' you know that HIV and AIDS are a major problem all over the Metro areas, Newark, New York, South Carolina, North Carolina, and Atlanta is all at high rates."

Kaleem was shocked about all the wisdom Queen had just unloaded on him. He was feeling hurt.

Mr. Devil began to speak again. *"Kaleem fuck that bitch! You can get any hoe you want. Fifteen years, c'mon, you see how beautiful and sexy she is!"*

"Shut the fuck up right now," Kaleem thought.

"Nah, you shut the fuck up!" the Devil demanded. *"What if you had got her in the bed and you caught the package? You still feeling her ain't yo?, Tender dick nigga. Just like Ta'Rod said, 'your head fucked up,'"*

"Give me a break,"

"You want her that bad? That you know she got that shit! What is the world coming to? I'm your partner homie. Let's get the hell out this joint,"

"Yeah, I guess you're right," Kaleem said, giving what he said some thought. "You still want me to take you to your car?" he asked Queen.

"If you will, I hope you understand,"

"Right now my head is fucked up, and I am angry that I played myself," Kaleem said. "I have something to do back over the way, can you tell Ms. Inez we leaving."

"Sure, before I do, I want you to know if things were different it would be a gift to be a part of your life. I'll be right back," Queen said sadly and walked off.

"I hope you enjoyed the food Kaleem," Ms. Inez said as she came out the room.

"I sure did. It was great. I appreciate it, take care of yourself."

"You both remember in this fast pace world, know that the power of God and prayer is awesome. In all circumstances, we give thanks to God. The best friend is a praying friend,"

"Ain't that right, Queen?"

"Yes, mama,"

"Whatever God does is for the best," Inez repeated.

"Bye, Ma. I will call you later."

"Bye, Ms. Inez," Kaleem said, giving her a hug.

"Love you both, God bless."

CHAPTER 22

Queen finally broke the silence during the ride back to Newark. "Kaleem, my mom's don't know anything about my sickness. I do appreciate if you don't say anything to her."

Kaleem noticed an unmarked car tailing him. *"Damn of all times to fuck with me, what a day, what a damn day."* he thought. Reluctantly Kaleem continued their conversation, "I need to be upfront with you as well, Queen,"

"What's that?"

"I'm a drug dealer, and right now I have a police car following us,"

"I knew you sold drugs a few months now. I hold you in my heart still."

"Well, right now, I can hit a couple of turns and you can jump out. I don't know what they are up to over here,"

"I want to stay just in case you need me to help,"

"You sure? They can be assholes at times,"

"I'm sure,"

"I don't know when he's going to pull me over. Put this phone in your pocketbook, the code is 0907; only two people have that number so make sure you answer it. If you miss the call, call them back. Don't let anyone see you doing this." he told her and then went on to say, "the car must be running with the passenger seatbelt connected.

Then push the air conditioner button once," When he pressed the button, the dashboard raised up, revealing his stash box; he picked his .40-Caliber up and put it inside, closing the stash when done. "It's about fifteen or twenty grand in there," he told Queen, "just in case you have to bail me out or something. Now, are you still sure?"

"No drugs?" she asked.

"Nah, no drugs at all,"

Queen didn't want to leave Kaleem hanging dry, so she decided to ride it out. Furthermore, she was enjoying the rush. Being in the middle of some action didn't seem to scare her.

"You know they may interrogate you."

"I know Kaleem, I ain't a snitch!"

After three more police cars pulled up, they turned on their lights. "Make sure you put your hands where they can see them," he told her as he began to pull over.

Just as he was pulling over the black Crown Victoria, cut in front of his car. "Hands up, get your hands up!" Six police jumped out guns drawn yelling.

"Cut the car off! Hands out the window, now!" one police yelled with authority.

"Do as they say and I love you, Queen!"

That statement cut into Queens' heart like a knife. Before she could respond, one cop was at the driver's window. "If you breathe, I'ma blow your head off! Out the car nice and easy," another cop demand.

"Handcuff them," said another.

"What's going on?" Kaleem asked.

"Shut the fuck up!" the big cop replied. "Dispatch, hook me up direct to Director Baye of Newark, please,"

"Ten-four,"

"Baye here, Hello,"

"Yes, Mr. Baye, this detective McClaen of Jersey City Police Department. We got your suspect from the BOL (Be On the Lookout) he has a female with him."

"I appreciate your help. I don't need the girl, get her name and she can go. Take Kaleem to Hudson County and we will take it from there. I owe you one, buddy."

"Okay, no problem."

They handcuffed the both of them and put them in separate police cars. McClaen ruffled through Queens's pocketbook as the others searched the car. McClaen opened the police car door where they had Queen sitting. "You going down for a long time," he told her. Queen sat there and didn't respond. "How did you get yourself tied up with scum like this? He just told my officers the drugs they found just now in the car are yours!"

Queen thought, *"How could he, or this lying cop playing me?"*

"Is there anything you want to tell me, 'cause he is over there singing like a bird," McClaen said.

Queen finally broke her silence. "That's funny, he told me he could not sing," Queen stated sarcastically. "When can I call my attorney?"

"Never!" he slammed the door.

The officers huddled up talking. They diverted from their meeting and jumped into the vehicles. One was driving the Honda.

When they pulled in front of Hudson County, Queen thought, *"You can't breakdown, girl."* Her conscience spoke to her: *"Yeah, many people that ain't know nothing go to jail. You heard the cop say, 'he is blaming it all on you.'"*

The Holy Spirit took over, *"Have faith, I will never leave you. I will give you what you need I know your heart."*

When they walked Kaleem pass the car, Queen blew a kiss to him as he disappeared into the building. "This is your last chance," the officer told her.

"I told you, I don't know anything, for the last time,"

"Don't get caught slipping, sexy, the keys in his car; you're free to leave now."

"Thanks," Queen jumped in the Accord and took off.

* * *

Queen left a message for an attorney friend, Mr. Cooper, asking him to look into Kaleem's situation. Then she called Cookie...

"Hello," Cookie answered.

"Hey, Cookie, where you at?"

"I'm on Summerset. Why? You don't sound too good, Queen,"

"I'm not. I need ya' help, I'm in Jersey City on my way back to Newark now. I will be over there in twenty,"

"I'ma be outside." Cookie hung up.

Queen drove like she had a race car, she handled the five-speed clutch Accord well.

Beep, Beep... She pulled up blowing the horn.

"Damn, Queen, who whip you rocking? This shit is right word is bond, girl,

"Get in. Girl, I was with Kaleem, we had gone to church, then to my mother's house for breakfast, and when we left police pulled us over,"

"Damn," Cookie replied.

"Plus, I told him I am infected,"

"What! What did he say?"

"He snapped, what you think. I broke it down to him that that's why I didn't lead him on, then I gave him a better understanding about the sickness. I also told him that I couldn't see him anymore then this all jumped off!"

"So he getting that paper like I said?"

"Yep, I got to put his car in the garage and get mine from the church parking lot,"

"You ain't going to be sporting this fly shit?"

"Nah, I don't want people to see me driving it,"

"What you do when the Narc's pulled y'all over?"

"What you think, I used my Fifth Amendment the right to keep my mouth closed!" they both laughed.

* * *

Baye, along with another detective arrived at Hudson County to question Kaleem.

"Well, well, well, Kaleem, your show is over now! We know you called that hit on Big Jay and his gang. The girl from Thirteenth Street worked for you too! Now if you want us to help you, you have to help us."

"Listen, I didn't call no hit. Where I'm from you got to do your own job," Kaleem spat.

"Now you listen you little bastard, you're barking down the wrong tree, I'm gonna end your career unless you can pull it off behind bars."

"What about my phone call?" Kaleem asked, ignoring what he just said.

"What phone call?" Baye turned to leave out and slammed the door behind him.

The two Hudson County Correction Officers had come and told Kaleem to change out into the jail uniform. By the time they came back, he was dressed. "Here is your location: C-500 room 132 bottom. Enjoy your stay," the C.O said sarcastically.

"They on some bullshit, it is what it is." Kaleem thought.

The doors opened to C-Pod. The officers stayed inside the booth looking over the pod.

Door 132 slid open. "What's up?" a guy said, looking about in his early thirties. My name is Shake. Who you be?" he asked.

"Kaleem, what's good?"

"You from around here?"

"Nah, Brick City,"

"Newark?" Shake replied.

"Yeah, what's up?"

"I'm cool with y'all. It's some cats from Duncan and Curry Woods Projects don't want y'all on this pod. Now on A-500 pod they chill down there, they know down prison it get nasty.

"Man, that's the young boys shit. Niggas 'bout eating, getting that bacon, feel me?"

"That's what's up. I was just putting you down. Do you know any Johnson's, Webb's, or Mack's? They live in Newark and Irvington."

"Yeah, I know a few of them,"

"How about the Dixons or McKennith?"

"Yeah, I know them too. You got a homie from Hayes Home name Born and a guy name Haneef up here. All they do is work out all day long. I think that's why they holding it down."

"Damn this joker is on top of everything!" Kaleem thought.

"I only got six months to do, yo' my family name ring bells around here too, Washington's,"

"That's the business, I'm just waiting for a bail, and it's a wrap. They got me on safekeeping,"

"No safe keeping on this pod. They don't know what the hell they doing," Shake said. "What they charge you with, Kaleem?"

"Nothin' yet,"

"They just busting your balls,"

"What time we get out in the morning? They had me downstairs all that time,"

"Breakfast is about 6 a.m. I will show you your two homies. It's on you if you want to meet them or not,"

"Don't let the size fool ya', I put on for my city," Kaleem warned.

"Good night my brother lights out in five minutes," Shake explained.

"That's the business," Kaleem replied, trying to get comfortable.

* * *

Breakfast came fast. It was about one hundred people standing around looking hungry or crazy. Everyone was checking out the new kid on the pod, Kaleem. He plays the cut, back against the wall, watching whoever was watching him.

A few guys came with small talk trying to see if Kaleem was a Blood, Crip, God Body, Gee, etc. Neutral, as they kept it moving. "What's good homie? We from the Bricks too,"

"Where you from?" one guy asked.

"Scudder Homes!" Kaleem stated. "I'm born from Hayes Homes."

"Yeah, Peewee, and Fella got bacon when they were up. This my man, Haneef, from Nineteenth Street,"

"Doc is a good person, that was my dude," Kaleem said.

"That's what it's hitting fo'. You need something get at me." Haneef said. "We 'bout to work out you want in?"

"Nah, I'm straight."

* * *

Queen knew it was time to call her attorney friend back, she dialed his office. "Hello, Cooper's Law firm, may I help you?"

"Hi, is Mr. Cooper in?"

"Yes, he is, may I ask who is calling?"

"Ms. Mack,"

"Please hold."

"Hello, Mr. Cooper, speaking, how can I help you?"

"Hello, Mr. Kevin Cooper,"

"Queen, I know that sweet voice from anywhere. How are you?" he asked.

"Just fine, I wanted to find out about a friend."

"Yes, yes, I got on that first thing this morning after I got your message. He is in safekeeping at Hudson County. He doesn't have a bail. Is someone after him, or is he a snitch?"

"No, I doubt that,"

"They are dragging him then," he stated. "So, Queen, are you married yet?"

"Not yet Kevin,"

"Queen, you know I've always wanted to make you mine. Why don't you swing by for lunch?"

"Not right now, but I appreciate your help,"

"No problem. Call me sometimes,"

"Thanks again, bye." They hung up.

"Girl, what you gonna do now?" Cookie asked Queen.

"Wait 'til he call,"

"You need to eat, Queen,"

"Not right now,"

"I will fix you something just in case,"

"Thanks, Cookie,"

"That's what girls are for," replied Cookie.

* * *

"Lockdown, lockdown all units!" were the words that echoed through the dorm. "Everybody to your rooms!"

"This some bullshit, using the phone is dead now." Kaleem thought.

"Man, how long this shit last?" Kaleem asked Shake.

"Just a couple of days, if we lucky,"

* * *

After two days of not hearing from Kaleem and the jail wasn't telling her anything, Queen was thinking of a million things at once. *"Do Kaleem hate me now? Will he look at me differently? Will we still be friends?"* Queen knew she would be better off not seeing Kaleem anymore. *"Only if things were different,"* Queen imagined.

* * *

It has been two days since Kaleem been in Hudson County. The jail was locked down due to a water main break. First day back out there rooms, Kaleem went right to the phone to call Queen.

"Hello," Queen answered.

"You have a collect call from, 'Kaleem', at the Hudson County Detention Center, press one to accept or press seven to decline, this call will be monitored and recorded, thank you."

"Hi, Kaleem, how are you?" Queen asked excitedly.

"I'm good,"

"Why you just calling?"

"Long story, listen, Queen, I need you to call an attorney. He is located in Hoboken, New Jersey, Mr. DeValle,"

"Okay, Kaleem, I also checked with an attorney that I know, he said you have no charges and no bail,"

"They fuckin' with me hard,"

"What about visits?" Queen asked.

"Hopefully, I won't be here. Did I get any calls yet?"

"Not yet,"

"Queen, these phones are recorded, so I'm not making them a record deal, got me?"

"Yes, I feel ya',"

"So, you stealing my words, huh?"

"Somewhat," she replied.

"Is the whip put up?"

"Done already,"

"Good, I will get at you when I can, Queen,"

"Okay, be safe." the phone hung up.

CHAPTER 23

The next day 9:00 a.m.

Click, click,

The doors to the cells unlocked. "You guys have rec this morning!" The officer yelled over the intercom.

Kaleem went straight to the phone. *"This some bullshit, she not picking up,"* he said to himself. He tried again at 10 a.m. still no answer.

"Kaleem Ward, visit. In room 132 you have a visit." said the C.O.

"Damn, yo' people on top of shit," Shake said. "Go to the wing door and the C.O will let you out."

"That's what it's hitting for," Kaleem stated and left the pod. He was wondering who was coming to see him.

He entered the visitation room and observed the other inmates and visitors. The visiting room had long bench cushion seats set about four feet apart. The room was well lit and had about five or six vending machines, they had the children's attention.

"What's your name?" the officer asked.

"Kaleem Ward,"

"Look, you get one hug and kiss at the beginning of your visit and the same at the end. Don't overdo it or your visits will be terminated. You understand?"

"I got ya',"

"Take a seat at number seven, please."

Silence landed upon the room as Queen entered. She was rocking a pair of beige leather pants by DKNY, a white wool sweater, and black Nine West Boots that set off the outfit. She walked with power and smoothness. Surely, she had every making of a Ms. America.

"Hi, Kaleem," Queen said, opening her arms to embrace him.

"Hello," he gave her a bear hug and then kissed her on her soft wet lips. *"Damn."* he thought to his self.

"You caught me off guard, Kaleem."

"Forgive me, it just seems natural,"

"After they told me you can have visitors. I came right down to visit you,"

"I appreciate that to the fullest. You a show-stopper, you're looking so good, Queen.

"C'mon, stop it, Kaleem,"

"Nah, real talk, you can feel the covetous women hating. The men are spellbound. They desire you as well…"

"Enough about them," she cut him off. "Mr. DeValle the attorney said he will get you out sometime today if everything goes well. He also said this cost five grand and to retain him will be twenty. You need me to do anything else?"

"Yes. Queen, I want you to absorb what I'm about to drop on you. What I have to offer you is my heart. I know you are my soul mate and you may have heard it a thousand times, but I'm willing to stand by your side, no matter what may come our way. I realize that no one can make me happy. I'm always thinking of you. In our conversations, the way I feel when I'm around you, just your presence gives me chills. You excite me like that,"

"But, Kaleem, I am feeling you as well, but I am so afraid. I would never want to hurt you. I mean, I can't do the things you deserve as a man," Tears began to fall from her deep green eyes.

Kaleem was getting up to hug Queen again, "Number seven have a seat, please!" one of the C.O's said.

"See what I mean, I'm ready to get this over with being in this County."

A small smile showed on Queen's face. "Baby, it is what it is," Kaleem told her. "I just want you to know, I used to say, 'I would never be with a woman that was infected with AIDS or HIV,' now I can never say that again. Queen, I want to be with you for the rest of my life!"

The Devil jumped in. *"You one dumb motherfucker. You giving up everything, even your life for some ass. Why don't you just shoot yourself in the head?"*

"Devil, you been riding my ass long enough, go fuck yourself,"

"No you're gonna wish you fucked yourself," the devil replied.

"I don't care what people may think or say! It's about you and me, Queen,"

"Kaleem, AIDS is like playing Russian roulette you're just waiting to die. I pray one day they will find a cure,"

"How about becoming an activist for AIDS?"

"That would be nice. So many people need to be educated. This virus cannot be seen. It has no color. It doesn't care what race you are or how much money you have, nor where you live. It takes anybody it can, young or old! They are the ones that seem to have it going on. The handsome men, nice bodies, cash flow up, the Benz, and house. He doesn't tell any of his sex partners he has AIDS! You also have the women that can win any beauty pageant. She has a figure eight body. I mean simply desirable. She has been giving her goodies away just 'cause she gets paid. She also has the package. People must cherish how valuable life is,"

"I agree with you, Queen. My soul cries out for you,"

"But, Kaleem,"

"Allow me to continue, Queen. I never knew how to love. You have opened doors in my life I never knew I had. Will you loan me your heart? Will you embrace my pain I gathered over the years? Please, don't view me as being soft or weak. Can we see life as one? How can't I appreciate a woman of your caliber? I have not even made love too. Your touch speaks volumes of love, affection, compassion, and understanding. You will be my Aphrodite (my goddess of love and beauty),"

Queen was shocked about the way Kaleem was putting it down to her. "You don't understand I want you too, it's just that…"

"No, I do understand. Allow me into your world…"

"Visitation is now over. All visitors, please exit at this time." a voice came over the speaker interrupting Kaleem.

When Kaleem stood up and gave Queen a hug, his manhood rose to the occasion, pressing against her soft thigh. They locked lips and began kissing.

Queen stopped, sadly saying, "I'm feeling lite headed and weak. I will see you later."

"Blessings see you soon," Kaleem replied.

Queen made her way out of the visiting room with all eyes on her. Kaleem admired her walk until she was out of sight.

* * *

After returning to the pod, Kaleem could still feel Queens's presence. Looking in her eyes, he placed his self into her hurt and pain, because he wanted so much to be in her life.

"How was your visit?" Shake inquired.

"It was penetrating!"

"Huh?" Shake implied, with a questionable look on his face.

"It was good, brah; I go in front of the judge today,"

"That's what's up,"

Mr. Devil spoke, *"I can't believe you kissed her! What about you getting infected? Damn love is that powerful, I never loved anybody. After all, we been through. There is so much still waiting for us to pop off. I can't see how you can imagine living without me yo',"*

"I'm tired of not knowing when I will get my wig pushed back. Jail will be forever, I wouldn't be doing nothing with my life. I got problems after problems. All I wanted was to live a normal life with someone that loves me for me," Kaleem thought.

"So I guess you on the Jesus trip now?" Mr. Devil told him.

"You can say, Jesus or Allah,"

"Go ahead and let her give you AIDS. That's what you want?"

The Holy Spirit spoke, *"Do you really think that the Devil has your best interest at hand? He loves destroying lives I love saving them. Queen is God's child no matter what sickness she may have. You see everybody in life will need someone. That's just how I made it. I have carried you this far because I have plans for your life. You see, my plans go much farther than yours. Listen while I explain to you what a woman looks for in a man! A leader, a King, she seeks unity, purpose, creativity, self-determination, values, morals and authenticity. He will achieve, protect, and serve her. He is loyal, romantic, fun and shows physical attention to her. Their energy must connect. She sees him facing challenges without having any doubt, that he will complete his mission. They will go through storms together. He is a good listener. He will lift her up when she is down, encouraging, and loving her. Follow me now I don't want to lose you. A man needs to know what a man is in order to be one! He needs to know who he is! Not just his race, age, and gender; his foundation must be built on love. If not, he will hate and the Devil will be his best friend. A man will be in tune with self. He is righteous, truthful, respected, honored, loved and a mentor. He will comfort any psychological barriers that may hinder him such as abuse, drugs, neglect, low self-esteem, and poor attitudes. He will focus on growth and is always open to knowledge. His conduct will show who he is in life. I put the spirit of love in your heart,"*

"Why?" Kaleem questioned.

"Because I Am love and you are mine! You need not be afraid of where you are going when you know I am going with you," said God through the Holy Spirit.

[167]

"Yo! Kaleem! They callin' you for court. You must be in another world,"

"That's the truth," Kaleem was zoned out.

"If they give you a bail you will come back here and then leave," Shake stated.

"Okay, let me go see what it's hitting fo'."

* * *

Kaleem waited in the holding room at court until his name was called, "Ward, step out, please, hands in front," Kaleem hands were handcuffed in front of him. "Walk right this way into the courtroom, sir," the C.O said.

"Excuse me, Mr. Ward,"

"Yes, I'm your attorney, Jose De Valle. How are you feeling this day?"

"I feel like I'm ready to get out of here,"

"I agree with you. We have a good Judge that hates how the system plays their dirty games. Did they give you any tickets?"

"Nah,"

"Any drugs or weapons involved?"

"No,"

"'Cause they got you charged with assault, resisting and eluding police,"

"That's some bullshit, none of that happened. They had two homicide detectives come question me from Newark last week,"

"Did you get their names?"

"I know one of them was, Baye,"

"He must have a personal interest in you, he is a big man over in Newark," Mr. De Valle replied.

"All rise, please. Judge Alexus Cokley presiding," said the court officer.

"Good afternoon," said the judge. "Please be seated," she continued, "We had a late start today, but we will do what we can. First case, please,"

"Hello, Judge, my name is Mr. Dillard and I will be representing the state today, against Mr. Ward, on five charges. Two assaults on a police officer, two resisting arrests, and one eluding police,"

"Okay is his lawyer present?"

"Yes, Hello, Judge Cokley, I like your new hairstyle,"

"Thank you,"

"Your Honor, for the record, my name is Jose De Valle and my client Mr. Ward pleads not guilty to the bogus charges against my client. The charges were made up to hold my client until Newark detectives came to speak with, Mr. Ward,"

"Go ahead, Mr. Dillard,"

"The officers pulled Mr. Ward over in a black Honda Accord with a female passenger. We have reason to believe Mr. Ward is a major drug dealer in the Newark area and trying to start now in Jersey City,"

"Hold on, hold on a minute now," stated the judge. "Was any drugs found?"

"No, Your Honor,"

"Where are the medical records of the injuries?"

"I don't have them at this time, Your Honor," said Mr. Dillard.

"May I offer, judge that no ticket was issued to my client nor was the car impounded," Mr. De Valle added.

"Mr. Dillard," the judge said. "If you have any more cases as this one, please don't waste any more of the courts time and money. Mr. Ward, I don't know if the drug dealing part is true or not, but there is no evidence at all concerning the charges I have before me. Mr. Ward, it's a shame that society can't trust the officials they pay taxes for, to be honest. The judicial system is made to break a person's spirit. The person must want to rehabilitate his or herself if they want to advance in life. It's sad that so many are falling short. All charges are dropped against the defendant today."

"But, Your Honor…" said Mr. Dillard.

"That will be my ruling. Next case!"

"Thank you, Your Honor," said Mr. De Valle.

"Thank you, Judge," Kaleem said.

"Good luck with your life, Mr. Ward!"

"Man, am I ready to go,"

"I bet you are. How did you hear about me?"

"Let's just say you know a couple of people that I know," Kaleem told him smiling.

"That's good to know. Is this a current address so you can get your mail? I need to send you out a contract,"

"Yeah, I will get it,"

"Okay, Kaleem, take care. Here are few business cards if you know anyone that needs my help, feel free to give them one. Call me if you need anything,"

"I appreciate it, Mr. De Valle,"

"Not a problem as soon as they process your paperwork you will be gone."

* * *

Kaleem was back in his cell waiting for his release.

"Shake, take care of yourself, and thanks for the input,"

"I'm an old head. I keep it real, baby."

"What size are those shoes you got, Shake?"

"They are a ten, why?"

"This my second time wearing these Jordan's you can have them if you want,"

"Hell yeah, that's good looking, Kaleem, word!"

"If you ever over on the Bricks get at me. I wrote my number down on this paper…"

"Ward, pack up. Ward, room 132,"

"That's you," said Shake. "Blessings and respect my brother."

"Same here," Kaleem responded, shaking his hand.

Kaleem got his clothes and changed. *"I can't wait to wash this jail smell from my body,"* he thought.

When he made it downstairs, Queen was standing there looking lovely with her beautiful smile. "Hi, handsome, I thought you might want a ride," she told him as he approached her.

"I would ride to the moon with you, beautiful,"

"I'm glad you're out of that place. Your attorney called me to let me know you were being released,"

"Yeah, he good at what he do,"

"Where do you need to go?" she asked.

"I need to get my car. Do you have my phones with you?"

"Of course, here they are,"

"Thank you. I'm sorry you had to go through this mess. They didn't harass you too much that day, did they?"

"The one cop came back to the car I was in and said that they found a lot of drugs in your car, and you said it was mine. Then he said you were singing like a bird,"

"I can't even sing?"

"That's what I told him too," they both laughed.

"What are you doing tonight?" Kaleem asked.

"I am going to work,"

"I appreciate your help. How much I owe you?"

"That's what friends are for to help each other in times of need, right?"

"Yes, but like I explained to you I want to be your man. I am in love with you, Queen, and nobody else can make me happy but you,"

"Kaleem, I'm gonna give you some time and let's see if you still feel the same. I'm surely going to pray on this. Only God knows what is in store for the both of us,"

"I agree with you, I have been thinking. I've been fighting my conscience and my spirit tells me to go with my heart. And that's for me to live my life with you, Queen,"

"Your words dig deep into my soul. We have a strong chemistry and I can't stop what God does! Here are your keys. When a sister gives a man her house keys, she had better have his as well,"

"You ain't saying nothing but a word,"

"Let me get to work, Kaleem. I'll call you later,"

"Okay, one more kiss before you leave, baby,"

Queen leaned over and gave Kaleem a nice soft kiss. He felt like he was flying. *"I better keep my seatbelt on,"* he thought. "I'll call you later," he told her as she got out the car.

* * *

Kaleem's first call was to, Santos. "What's good, boss?"

"Welcome, my friend. I want you to know it's been good business with you, Kaleem. The alphabet boys are asking questions and it's time to close down. You never know how long they been around or who they know my friend, see. I think you should invest your money and come clean,"

"I was thinking the same thing, boss. I'm ready to settle down, the game is dead,"

"What Ta'Rod doing?" Santos asked, knowing he would go do his own thing.

"I got to get at him. His motto is money over everything so I have to cut ties,"

"Kaleem at times, no matter how much money you got you still ain't happy. Money makes you forget what really makes you happy in life. Peace and happiness can't be bought, that comes from within. That is, when you learn the true meaning of love. Love when you have only your heart to give. Love will walk, run, or crawl to reach its destination! Something's you can just feel. Kaleem, you need to come meet Camarie,"

"Who is, Camarie?"

"Camarie, is the name of my super yacht. It has one master bedroom, four guest rooms, and two baths. It holds over ten thousand gallons of gas and three thousand gallons of water. It has a kitchen. Even if you don't like the heat and sun like that, you can chill with air-conditioning all day long. I named her after a sweet little girl,"

"Damn, boss, she sounds beautiful,"

"Let's say Puffy has a nice yacht no doubt. Mine is the real life volume. You won't be able to reach me any longer my friend so it's been good, no?"

"It's been good, boss,"

"Blessings and respect to you, Kaleem,"

"Loyalty my boss, always," They both hung up the phone.

"Damn, that yacht got to be at least twenty million! This shit is crazy." Kaleem thought after he hung up.

* * *

Finally, Kaleem got to Ta'Rod. "Yo' my nigga, I see you still in one piece. What's good?" Ta'Rod said, embracing him.

"I'm Gucci, shit is, FBI hot right now!"

"What! Why you say that?"

"Santos got word and he shut down the business,"

"Fuck it, we just gotta find another connect,"

"Nah, Ta'Rod, you ain't hearing me. If they on him, plus with this shit jumpin' over here, we on fire right now! Feel me?"

"Kaleem, I'm gonna die behind this shit all I have is me. I have no family. The streets are my life,"

"You can take your money and do something legal,"

"Like what?" Ta'Rod asked as if it was something impossible.

"Open a club. You like playin' yo' music! Or, give it to them boys when they come, 'cause their coming!"

"So what's up with you? What you gonna do?"

"I'ma lay and build a future with, Queen, she is my soul mate. She is sick and I'ma take care of her the rest of her life,"

"What you mean, sick?"

"She has the virus,"

"What!" Ta'Rod exclaimed. "You got to be joking,"

"Why would I play like that?"

"Damn, my dude, you must really be in love to be willing to give your life for her,"

"She helped me change my mindset and understand that anyone with HIV or AIDS are still people. Death will come to all of us in life. I sure would stand by anyone in my family if they had the disease,"

"That's what its hittin' fo', I see yo' mind is made up so I got to respect that,"

"Yeah bro, I love the woman. I got to run I'll get at you later,"

"That's what it do homie."

* * *

Dionne is one of Queen's girlfriends that works for Transit. She stopped by the hospital to see and talk to, Queen. "Girl, I've been looking for you all week. Why yo' red ass ain't been calling me lately?" Dionne asked Queen.

"I been tied up working,"

"Well, this is what I heard about my girl, Queen. Word is, you been seeing a big-time dealer name, Kaleem. The popo's are looking for him and the Young Mafia Gang looking for him too. They say Kaleem don't play no games when it comes to his business. So what's really good? You been seeing him or what?" Dionne held no punches, and got straight to the questions, being nosey.

"Yeah, Dionne, we been out a few times and I am feeling him. He has shown me nothing but respect,"

"Respect!" Dionne yelled. "He's gonna get killed if the cops don't get him first. Girl, you better stop seeing him now if you love your life, you hear me." Dionne always played the miss know it all in their friendship.

"Yeah, I hear you, Dionne; I'm in love with him,"

"Did y'all fuck?" she asked bluntly.

"No!"

"Did he eat ya' coochie?"

"No!"

"Well, how in the hell you in love, girl? You just talking,"

"Dionne, my heart tells me this is the man for me, and I ask God to allow me to know it,"

"You make sure he knows about, Mother – Dionne because I got my pistol in my closet waiting for somebody too,"

"I'll be sure to tell him,"

"You know you my girl and I love you, Queen,"

"Love you too, Dionne. Let me get back to work before I be moving in with you." Queen said laughing.

"Yeah, take ya' ass back to work. Girl, I walk around my house naked too much for girl company!"

"On that note, I'm gone. Too much information bye, girl,"

"Call me later," Dionne told her walking off.

"I wonder if Kaleem would stop selling drugs. All I want is a basic life where both of us are happy. I want him for who he is and how he makes me feel inside and out," Queen got chills just thinking about him. *"The way he gave me those kisses had me fluttering with the downpour that sensually came out while I was in his embrace. I just love that man I don't care what they say."*

CHAPTER 24

Queen went to grab some lunch at the café inside the hospital. "Oh my God!" she said, seeing Natalie, her longtime co-worker. "Hi, Natalie, I saw you sitting over here like you just got finish crying. Is there anything I can do to help, sweetie?"

"Hi, Queen, I'm just trying to pull myself together, I checked my husband's, Michael computer the other night and found out, he has been having an affair!"

"Pull yourself together, Natalie. You pray about the situation,"

"No. I am so hurt, Queen,"

"I understand that's your husband,"

"I'm going to make him pay for hurting me like this. I'm the one that laid up and had three kids for him; I'm the one who took care of him after his accident. I don't do nothing but go to work and back home. What's wrong with me?"

"Natalie, don't blame yourself. It wasn't you that cheated,"

"I should take everything he got,"

"Would that make things any better?"

"No, but it damn sure won't make things easy for him!"

"Now you got a point there," they both got a laugh in, "I won't tell you what to do, girl, but go to God in prayer and ask him to show you what to do. I mean only you know if the marriage is worth saving,"

"Thanks, Queen, I will do that. You have the right words at the right time,"

"Natalie, you know, anything we have ever talked about always stay between us,"

"I respect and appreciate you, Queen,"

"No problem. Now if you decide to take all his money, don't forget my cut," Queen stated jokingly.

"Now, you know you can get anything from me,"

"I'm just joking, girl. I will be praying for you and Michael, also read your Bible,"

"Okay,"

"I have to get to work call me if you need me." Queen told her and walked off, and thought, *"God, it can only be you that direct my life, it must be you that sent Kaleem into my life. Someone that loves me for who you made me; someone that understands that you, God is the Father of us all; that you created every one of us. Lord, please guide the both of us and keep us safe from harm or danger."* She felt Kaleem's presence just from thinking of him. She felt the joy as a teenager. *"I can't wait to be with him. Maybe they will find a cure for me and we can be a regular couple. Even with him knowing the consequences, and still willing to share my life. The bottom line is that it is show and tell time! I know I love this man, I guess I'm crazy in love. Matter of fact, let me text him something,"*

"Hey handsome I am thinking 'bout you and I can't believe what you do to me. A deluge comes even when you're not around. I love it! LOL, Queen,"

"I have to fix him dinner one day. I got to show him, momma showed me how to throw down in the kitchen as well." Growing in love with someone that loves you back is priceless. *"I know only if we both are on the same accord, our relationship will work."*

There's not an hour that goes by that, Queen is not thinking about that man. She was true to her love for, Kaleem.

After Queen's shift was over, she thought, *"Damn, Kaleem still hasn't replied to my text. I hope he is all right and everything is fine."*

As Queen walked to her car, she couldn't get him off her mind. She sat in the car waiting for it to warm up. *"It's chilly tonight,"* she thought.

* * *

When Queen made it home, she was still worried that Kaleem didn't call back. She kept looking at her phone, however, didn't want to sweat the man she wanted to be with.

She ran her some hot bath water, with bubbles and Oil of Olay bath oil, lit some DOLCE & GABBANA candles, undressed, sat in the tub and relaxed her state of mind as she soaked her body for forty-five minutes. She enjoyed looking at herself naked, thanking God for making her the way he has.

Queen learned how to please herself, being that she refused to let any man touch her in fifteen years, she became close friends with her pleasure zone. She learned that only inside women chemicals in their brain give off oxytocin and dopamine during orgasm. So she mastered the G-Spot and clitoris. She neglected to use a dildo. Thinking that one day, she will be able to feel the real deal inside of her pleasure zone. Queen is hot blooded, her vagina stayed wet and juicy. She always kept panty liners in her pocketbook just in case she got too wet. After freshening up, Queen went to bed thinking about the questions she wanted to ask Kaleem. *"I will be his one day. I will tear him apart whenever that day does come. Or if it ever comes. I have to get some rest,"* she thought.

Knowing she had a hair appointment early at Sybil's Beauty parlor in Vauxhall up Springfield Avenue in Maplewood. Queen had been going there ever since her friend from the church, Dorothy opened it up. It was a nice family type setting and the girls did great work.

"What will I wear in the morning? Let me take my behind to sleep and think about my man." she thought. She said her prayers and went to sleep.

* * *

"Aww, fuck!" Kaleem looked at his phone to see he had ten text messages, one being from Queen. When he read her text, a smile came across his face. He sat thinking how he wanted to respond to her text… *"What!"* he said to his self after seeing a text from Ta'Rod, that read,

"Yo', word out, Young Mafia Gang looking to put you six feet under. I say we put Haas on Big Jay!"

A text from, Dawg, read,

What it do brah, hit me up when you can, I don't want to run out of gas.

A text from, Cheryl, read,

"Hi, sweetie, what's up? It's gonna be a big party on the Island this weekend bring some of ya' friends over if y'all want to come. It will be full of women. Love you call me!"

A text from his momma read,

"I have not spoken to my son in four days. Do not forget you got a mother in Virginia. Love ya'."

Kaleem ate, got in the shower, and then hopped on the phone.

"If it ain't one thang it's another. I guess Big Jay thinks I made the call at the funeral home too. It is too late to be talkin'. What ya' gonna do when I come for you, Big Jay!" Kaleem thought.

Omar Poochie texted,

"Yo', nigga come check my fighters out on the weekend of the eighth. I got a middleweight that is the truth. My heavyweight quit on me in the third round last month, one big pussy! LMAO. Mo wants to talk to you too, you know ya' sister."

A text from, Angela, read,

"Having a seafood bash next month make sure you come down. And ya' moms can't wait to see her baby. Much love."

Lolesha text read,

"Hey, Kaleem just wanted to say hi. I'm in North Carolina now working my butt off. Luv u cuz, God bless."

After Kaleem checked all of his messages, he had to call them back. They always showed that unconditional love, no strings attached. *I guess that's that southern love!*

Kaleem had so much drug money in the apartment that he didn't even know how much it was. He hasn't used the money-counting machine in about eleven months. He just been counting the boxes, filling them up in stacks and keeping it moving. The FEDS got a dude from down D.C and got him for all his money. Kaleem knew he needed to get rid of his shit; he didn't want the FEDS eating off it. He sat thinking of ways for him to get out the game. *"Maybe I should get at Rob."* Rob, was a family member of, Kaleem. Rob used to run hard when he was in the game. He put all that behind him and got him a trucking company Called, 'Right On Trucking'; with trucks, running from state to state at all times. Kaleem knew he had to do something quick, fast, and in a hurry.

Kaleem turned on the music system in the house and bumped, Colonel Abram, *"Oh, oh, I'm trapped, Like a fool, I'm in a cage, I can't get out, You see I'm trapped, Can't you see I'm so confused? I can't get out,"*

Kaleem knew the whole song, he felt like, Colonel Abram, was speaking to him directly about his life. Trapped in life with a woman with AIDS, that he has never slept with; And inside a war, that only leaves bodies. He wanted to get out the street life. He thought, *"People will think I am a punk. That I'm scared. I don't want to give my life to the system, or have an early death if I don't have too. The hell with what people think. Their gonna talk regardless. People just want to use you for what you can do for them anyway. It's hard to find people that are real. I think that's the main reason I am in love with, Queen..."*

Here comes Mr. Devil again, *"Yo', man, you on some crazy shit now, look at all this cash around this house. You know how many people will kill to have this cash. Now you want to punk out! Look at all the other drug dealers that stayed in the game only thing happen to them was they lost everything, got an ass load of time, or were murdered! At least you can tell war stories when you go to jail. I'll still roll with you even in there, homie,"*

"You're right, if I keep rolling with you I will never ever have anything," Kaleem shot back to the Devil."

* * *

Sybil's Beauty Shop was crowded as always. The girls that work there does hair good.

"Hi, Queen," the receptionist said as Queen walked in.

"Hi, Honey,"

"I have an appointment with, Dorothy,"

"Sure do, got you right here. Go right to the shampoo area and let Channon wash all that lovely hair of yours."

"Hey, Dorothy, hi, Channon," Queen spoke.

"Hey, girl," Dorothy responded.

"Hey, Queen," Channon said.

"Queen, you are rolling with much more joy than I ever saw in you before, could that be coming from your friend I seen at church with you?" Dorothy asked.

"What friend?" Chantal questioned wanting to hear the juice.

"Not Queen! I have never seen you with a man, girl, I thought you had a woman," said Opal.

"If it ain't swinging, we ain't hanging," Queen responded.

"I heard that," Channon said.

"Y'all don't know what y'all missing," Opal told the ladies. Opal loved women; she always picked the wrong type of men. One day, she let her girlfriend talk her into getting her coochie ate. That was all it took.

"It's not about sex all the time," Dorothy stated.

"Speak for yourself," shouted Channon.

"I'm on yo' side, Channon," Opal said.

"Well, let me ask you ladies this," Dorothy continued, "can you be deeply in love with someone that you never had sex with?"

"Huh!" The girls looked at her as if she was from Mars.

"I find that to be true," Queen added.

"Why you think that?" Chantal asked.

"Because if the both of you are getting to know each other you will have a chemistry building if he's the one. I mean when he is on your mind day and night. When he isn't around and you get wet thinking about him to the point that you have small orgasms. When your vagina is pulsating every time he comes around and he has never even seen you naked!"

"Girl, where you find somebody like that?" Opal asked.

"The hell with that, I'll take his brother," yelled Channon. "He sounds like a keeper,"

"Aww, that just makes me want to stop having sex until I start getting treated like a woman instead of just a piece of meat," another lady in the shop said.

"Ain't no way he got ya' like that, girl," said Malika.

"I ain't lying," said Queen.

"To get me like that, he got to be working me inside and out, I run the show," said Tasha.

"Girl, I ran into this guy I've wanted to get with for years. Well, this nigga running around town talkin' about he did a Rambo on this good wet-wet I got, shit when he said he was finished, I said 'put ya' clothes back on, Boo, 'cause I didn't know you started!'"

"No, you didn't, Loise!"

"Yes the fuck I did, girl. He lucky that's all I did,"

Queen's phone started vibrating. A text from Kaleem came through. His ringtone was, Stevie Wonder, *'All I Do'*.

"I guess we know who that is," Channon said.

"I bet she wet now," said Opal. The shop started laughing aloud.

Kaleem's text read,

"Hello, beautiful, sorry I missed you last night. I was getting my rest for you. You got me open, girl, and that's without ever sexing you. Some say I'm crazy. Guess what, I love being crazy for you!"

"Okay, ladies this is what I'ma do; I will call him, put him on speaker, and ask him to explain if he knows what a woman should look for in a man,"

"Go head, girl, let's see is he the one," the ladies coached on the show.

Queen dialed Kaleem and put her phone on speakerphone. "Hey, Mr. Kaleem,"

"Hi, beautiful, how are you today?"

"I'm good,"

"I can only imagine,"

"I wanted to get your point of view on what a woman looks for in a man,"

"What a woman looks for in a man," Kaleem repeated. "A leader, a King, she seeks unity, purpose, creativity, self-determination, values, morals and authenticity. He will achieve, protect, and serve her. He is loyal, romantic, fun and shows physical attention to her. Their energy must connect. She sees him facing challenges without having any doubt, that he will complete his mission. Am I talking too much?" he stopped and asked.

"No, honey, only if you are finished,"

Kaleem continued, "They will go through storms together. He is a good listener. He will lift her up when she is down. You see a man needs to know what a man is to become one. And that can only be taught by other men! His foundation must be built on love. If he is in tune with self, he will respect others as well. He is righteous, truthful, respected, honor, loved, and a mentor. He will accept when he is wrong. He will confront any psychological barriers that may hinder him such as abuse, neglect, low self-esteem or a poor attitude towards life. He will focus on growth and is always open to knowledge. His conduct towards her will show it. Now I can only speak for what I will be for you."

Kaleem dropped a bomb on the whole beauty parlor. The shop was in silence.

"Hello, hello," Kaleem spoke into the phone.

"Sorry, I was lost in thought for a second," Queen told him.

"If you have time just hit me later,"

"Okay, be safe," Soon as Queen hung up, her phone went off again, it was, Kaleem, "Hello," she answered.

"One last thing, now a lot of women will settle for less, but that isn't what you're getting." he told her and then hung up.

"He is the man." Queen thought to herself. *"God you sure got a way of working things out."*

"Girl, if you don't want his deep voice, make me wet hell of a man, I'll take him off yo' hands," said Chantal.

"He can make me love men again," Opal said laughing.

"Sorry, girls, I think I'ma marry him before I let anybody take him!"

"You better, girl," Dorothy said as Queen sat in her chair. "I know you prayed on that situation?"

"I sure did. Plus, I got Dionne with her pistol," everyone laughed.

"Hi, Alnesa, where you been hiding?" Channon asked.

"You know the kids keep their father and me on the go all the time, girl,"

"I haven't seen Donna in a while, how is she doing?" Channon asked.

"Enjoying her grandkids, you know it is three of them now,"

"Yeah, I saw ya' brother baby; that boy looks just like him."

"I agree with you girl," said Alnesa.

"Queen, I can't see how you do it, girl, no sex in fifteen years! I bet you've been bought a couple of dildos," Opal said with a smile as the women laughed.

"No, honey, I don't do that. The only thing go up in this is when it's that time of the month and that hurts. I value my goodies that God gave me. When he, my husband that is, get this, he will need to cut me open just to get in," bragged Queen.

"Now that's tight," said Dorothy.

"You good, girl, I'll say that," replied Chantal.

"This looks nice, 'D'. Put me down for next weekend," Queen told her.

"Enjoy your hairstyle,"

"I will,"

"Your hair is growing so much," Dorothy compliment Queen, putting a smile on her face.

"Bye everyone, have a blessed weekend."

"Okay, you too," the shop replied.

"She is a good woman," Dorothy stated.

"God is surely carrying her," Channon replied.

"I'll tell you what; her friend sounds like he loves hard. And if his actions back up his words, that's what I will call a King all day long, girl," said Dorothy.

Everyone agreed.

CHAPTER 25

"Hello, can I speak to, Mr. De Valle,"

"Speaking,"

"Hey, Mr. De Valle, this is, Kaleem,"

"What can I do for you, Kaleem?"

"I have a friend that wants to give money towards a school. But he don't want his name involved,"

"Well, you know that's a tax write-off?"

"Yeah, but he ain't concerned with that. He wants to know how much it will take to make it happen."

"Where is the school that he wants to donate too?"

"No, he wants to build a school in Newark, Central Ward District,"

"What!" Mr. De Valle was shocked. "You got to be shitting me!"

"Nah, building it, he wants to have the residents from the area to be hired and help build it. After the school is built will the State fill the spots to run it with the teachers?"

"Yes of course; that will be major help that the people need. The state will jump on that," Mr. De Valle agreed. "Kaleem, do your friend know we are talking about millions of dollars? At least seven million,"

"Yeah, he will give you a little lead way in case anything comes up,"

"With this being for the kids, Kaleem, I'm willing to put my career on the line if your friend has a love for them like that," Mr. De Valle still thought it was a joke. However, he knew Kaleem was dead ass! "Well, I got…"

"Hold on! I don't need to know anything but that you're on top of this," Kaleem added as he cut Mr. De Valle off during his sentence.

"How soon will he be ready?"

"That will be as soon as you put everything together. In two weeks, I will speak to you in person and you will then have access to the cash so you can do what is all needed. I have two quotes I will never forget, 'You know loyalty takes you a long way' and 'Whatever God does is for the best',"

Mr. De Valle automatically knew that Kaleem was connected to Santos. Mr. De Valle knew it wasn't a game to be playing with that much cash. "I understand clearly. 'Loyalty,'" Mr. De Valle repeated.

"I will be in touch." They both hung up.

Mr. De Valle knew he had to put the money into a Swiss bank account and funnel it back as a non-profit, knowing it was cleaning up the money for a cause like this, a white-collar crime. *"The hell with it."* he thought, knowing he would pocket an easy million to the head. *"This will really be a great help to Newark,"* the lawyer thought.

* * *

Kaleem was trying to put everything in order. He was feeling that his life might end soon. He needed to get some cash down to his Aunt Gertrude and his mother to make sure they were set. They couldn't just use anybody's bank. There was no way he was letting them trap him off and take all this money, no way!

Kaleem started counting all his money to get the figures together. He wanted to hit up Elijah and let him know that, he was given up the streets. Hotrod was like a brother to Kaleem; they had a cool bond. One day while Hotrod was on a call with someone, that person didn't know that Kaleem was on the phone, Hotrod thought he clicked him off the line. The guy started talking about Hotrods black friend that he would see from time to time in Newark, that they didn't like him when they saw him in South Carolina. Kaleem; Hotrod told them if they didn't accept Kaleem, he wouldn't accept them. From that day, Kaleem would give his life for his white brother. Kaleem wasn't stuck on no color shit.

Kaleem thought about giving all his money away to help people. *"Damn. I don't care. With all this other stuff going on, somebody is coming after it, sooner or later. How can I change my life, serving people drugs, hurting so many people, and murder? I'm the worst of the worst,"* he thought.

The Holy Spirit spoke, *"You had to learn that material things could never make you happy. I have plans for you and my plans were not like yours. I have been carrying you for a long time, however, you never seemed to have paid attention. I forgave you for your sins when Jesus died on the cross! I love you because I Am your Father! No amount of money in the world can give you what I can,"*

"That's all good, but now Young Mafia Gang got a price out for my head," Kaleem thought. *"So, I gotta get them before they get me,"*

"Aight," the devil came out and said, *"now, that's what I'm talkin' 'bout. Put on that vest you brought, take both guns, and unload on, Big Jay. I knew you weren't gonna let them get away with that!"*

"Devil, you don't care about me, you never did!"

"I treat you like I treat the rest,"

"That's why I refuse to give you control of my life. And more, this relationship is over. Peace,"

"You will be back!" the Devil told him.

"That's what you think," Kaleem replied.

* * *

After Kaleem got his money boxed up in boxes of one million, he headed back down to Newark. He knew that if he took one million dollars for himself and managed it right, he could retire with fifty thousand dollars every year. He realized he could live better with less.

Big Jay had been riding around looking for Kaleem himself. He hit, Nye Avenue, Walnut St., Sunset St., Columbia Ave., Central Ave., Weequahic Ave., Vascur Ave., Parkview Ter. Lyons Ave., Clinton Place, Twelfth Ave., Orange, Ave., Park Ave., Orange St., South Orange Ave., and Eighteenth Ave., ready to make his AK-47 talk; cranking Lil Wayne, in his Land Rover, while smoking on a blunt.

Big Jay decided to go lay-up with his girl for the night. Wanting to relieve his fluid of love and joy inside of her, in other words, he just wanted to have sex.

* * *

Kaleem remembered that Jamillah was having a birthday party at the Ranch in Hillside. He knew he had to go show some love. He had been friends with the family for years and everyone thought that the both of them met their match. They enjoyed each other's company and always respected who they were to each other. He knew that the place was gonna be packed, Jamillah and her family were well loved by everyone and they had mad support. Kaleem wished he had got her a gift. It was too late, so he called the club owner, Strachie. "Hello,"

"Whopnin,"

"Yo', Strachie,"

"Wagwan bredren?"

"This Kaleem,"

"Yo', rude boy, what's happening? Respect,"

"Respect," Kaleem replied.

"What the blood clot goin' on with dem sayin' yo' got a price on ya' head? Yo' know me love ya' virgin. Me don't won't ya' dead seem!" Strachie told Kaleem.

"I'm good. You know jokers don't want to see me eat. Rude boy, you need to retire and go legit. The streets are dead. These pussy clots out here not gonna let you live. The game has changed, seem!"

"Yo', that's respect. But check it, I forgot all about Jamillah party and I want you to make sure she enjoy herself. I will cover a five hundred dollar tab.

"Strachie, listen, Jaheim is on his way to hang out with me for the night. We flying to Jamaica tomorrow afternoon,"

"'Nuf said, I got you. I'ma get him to do one song for her,"

"That's wonderful. Make it happen and let me know what I owe you. You know you me brother and noting can change that. You're like throwing a rock in a pond with the ruffle effect spreading love anywhere you go!"

"Respect, Strachie, love you, my brother. I have to finish handling things. Don't worry yourself, me got ya'. Be safe, respect." They hung up the phones.

Kaleem was still counting and boxing up his cash. He decided to chill and hit Newark tomorrow...

* * *

"So, you found ya' way to my place, huh?"

"I don't want to hear yo' mouth tonight, Sharonda!" Big Jay said with an attitude.

"What you mean tonight, it's two in the morning, Jay. You know I was waiting for the money to go to the mall today. Nah, you didn't even call a sister!

Big Jay lit up a blunt. He hadn't had any sleep in two days, he was beat. After taking a shower he fell asleep without even getting any goodies from, Sharonda.

It was about five a.m. and Sharonda was tired from looking at movies waiting to see if Big Jay would put her to

[195]

sleep. She had the meanest head game in her hood. This chick would suck the meat from a whole chicken without any hands!

"Why this damn," Sharonda said to herself after a light blew out. Just then, the TV blinked out. "This some bull-shit, Jay, Jay!" she tried to wake him up. "Wake yo' ass up!"

"Why you want look at TV or something?"

"I was until the power went out,"

"What!" Jay sat straight up. "Aww fuck…"

Bam!

The front door fell in, followed by the back door as well. Jay jumped out the bed to the sounds of FBI screaming. "Get on the floor!"

Butt naked both Jay and Sharonda lay on the floor. "We got this bastard now," said one agent. "You'll never see the streets again. You are being charged with, organized crime, King Pen, and gang relation, multiple murders, extortion, and kidnapping! You're going to sweetie."

Sharonda cried and yelled, "I got my kids. I don't know anything," Her heart rate doubled.

"Yeah, yeah, tell it to the judge. Handcuff them, throw a blanket around them, and let's get out of here,"

"We can't put nothing on?" Big Jay asked.

No one said a word as they marched out the house, all twenty of them. They hit three other spots at the same time, catching nine of Big Jay's gang all together.

"Aww, fuck," Big Jay said as they pulled up at the Federal building on Broad St. He knew the show as over. He didn't even give Sharonda with the 'blazing head' a second thought.

* * *

Kaleem had sat everything in place. Seven million was going to Mr. De Valle for the school for Kings and Queens, putting jobs back in the community, and of course his mom dukes and some family. *He was giving it all away.* The money that had blood, sweat, tears, and abuse all over it. *For the love of money!* Kaleem drove all over Newark knowing it could go down soon as he saw any member of the Young Mafia Gang or if they saw him first guns would be smoking. Moving low-key incognito, Kaleem toured 'Brick City' looking for anything strange so he could let off his nine and make change out of them. He rolled through, Red Bricks, Broadway Townhouse, Higher Courts, New Community, Georgia King Village, Baxter Terrace, Elizabeth Towers, Dayton St., Seth Borden, Academy Spyers, Pennington Courts, Prince St., Broome, Howard, Lincoln, Mercer St., Haze Home, High Park Garden, Steven Crane, Seventh Ave., Hill Manor, Collin Aides. Muhammad Ali Ave., Keer Ave., Bergen St., Fabyan Place, Park Ave, Mt. Prospect Place. Roseville Ave, Orange Ave, Sixteenth Ave, Bloomfield Avenue, Eighteenth St., and Clinton Ave., Stone Street, Sixteen Ave. and Avon. Kaleem burned out almost a tank of gas riding around.

He decided he wanted to go see Ms. Inez. He drove down to the gas station on Washington Ave. and Court St., and then stopped on Broad St. and grabbed a bottle of Johnny Walker Black. He was feeling very tense, so he enjoyed the smooth taste.

He dialed Ms. Inez. "Hello, Ms. Inez?"

"Yes, this is me,"

"This is Kaleem,"

"I know. How are you doing?" she asked.

"I'm good. I was gonna stop by around five o'clock if that's okay with you,"

"I will be here. You know whatever God does is for the best!"

"I can't forget that you tell me all the time! I will see you soon. You need anything?"

"No, I'm okay, Kaleem,"

"Okay, see you soon," he hung up.

"I got this nigga, now," Robo Cop said to himself. He had hooked up a unit he brought from the spy shop so he could tap phone lines. *"I should have been done this,"* he thought to himself. *"It doesn't matter how long he takes, I'ma head over that way now and wait on his ass in Jersey City."*

* * *

Queen had Kaleem open! He never dreamed that a woman would have him feeling the way she did. He had opened his eyes to see better things in life. Giving the money to open up a school was a major step. The money didn't control him anymore.

As Kaleem drove over to Jersey City to see Ms. Inez, he thought, *"I got to make dinner for Queen. I will show her how moms' taught me how to burn in the pots. Maybe some baked Red Snapper, Brown Rice, Broccoli, and some Baby Carrots. She can have me for dessert."*

He was feeling tipsy from the liquor; he wanted to make love to this girl so bad. No matter what, he wanted to spend the rest of his life with her anyway. Sex in his life was just that. Now he wanted to make love and grow inside a real true woman.

"*I might even go to East Orange to Brookers tonight and get my party on. I'm gonna see if the spirit works for me. The devil is not for me!*"

"*Shit, you'll be back,*" the Devil told him.

"*Good always over-ride bad,*"

"*You don't know what good is, nigga!*"

"*I'm learning what brings me peace in my life and fuckin' with you, it ain't gonna never happen,*"

"*Say what you want the proof will be in the time to come. When you run out of money or when those bills are too much for you to handle, or when you want to fight with God!*"

"*I ain't hearing you.*" Kaleem tuned the Devil out as he pulled up to Ms. Inez's house.

* * *

Knock, Knock,

"Hello, Ms. Inez,"

"Yes, who is it?" she said through the door.

"I'm Officer Scott. I am meeting Kaleem over here. He said he was on his way to see you,"

"Yes, he is," she stated still talking through the door.

When Ms. Inez looked out the window, she saw the unmarked car parked in front of the window, she also heard the police scanner she opened the door.

"How are you?" Robo Cop said.

"I'm blessed, thank God,"

"Yes, he told me he hadn't too long ago called you and he were coming to see you. I was in the area and we agreed to meet here,

"He isn't in any trouble is he?'"

"No, not at all, we are friends,"

"I'm glad to know that. Kaleem is a good young man. My hearing and my sight aren't that good anymore. I guess that's what happens when you get my age. How do you like being a police officer? Have a seat,"

"It gets dangerous sometimes, trying to keep the bad guys off the streets,"

"I see you're helping keep people safe. God always looks over good people and keep them safe,"

"Yes, he does. Can I use your bathroom, please?"

"Sure, it's right there," she pointed showing him the way.

"Thank you."

Robo Cop went into the bathroom and saw that the telephone line ran in there, so he cut the line. He then pulled out the half ounce of coke he took from Tyrone on Walnut Street last night. He put about a gram on a crisp twenty-dollar bill and broke the coke down into very fine fragments. He split it in half and like a vacuum cleaner; he finishes half of the cocaine. Then he went to the other side of his nose doing the same thing. Killing as many brain cells as he possibly could. He flushed the toilet, to make things sound good. Robo Cop brain was numb; only thinking about how much money he will have after making Kaleem tell where his stash house is.

Inez apartment only had two bedrooms facing the street. The kitchen and living room was up front, as you come in. Robo Cop knew Kaleem would be there in about twenty-five minutes if he were coming straight over. Robo had a different unmarked car so Kaleem would never think it was him. He couldn't wait to get this over with so he could go get a room, get high, and trick off with a prostitute. *"What a life."* he thought.

"You go to church, young man?" Inez asked when he came out the bathroom.

"Nah, too many phony people!"

"Well, you're never gonna find a perfect one. You go to hear the word of God. Do you believe in God, sir?"

"I'm not a spiritual person,"

"You know God has a way of doing things to show some of us who he is and what he does. The people who go in that hellfire will wish they took a different route in life. People make life hard,"

Robo Cop didn't want to hear all of that. "Yeah, I guess!"

"Where did you grow up?"

"Texas,"

"Did your grandpa have slaves?"

"Why?" Robo replied.

"Because you have a lot of hate and anger inside. What gets me, when people are racist and don't know why and then can't even explain it. They were taught it and never opened their brains to change the negative thinking. We all came from God!"

Inez never understood how stupid people could be in this world.

"Can I use your restroom again? I had too much to drink before I came here,"

"Go ahead, sir, not a problem,"

"This old ass lady talking to Fuckin' much. I have to hurry up. This nigga should be coming soon, " Robo Cop thought while in the bathroom scooping more cocaine onto a bill. He flushed the toilet and pushed his face into the coke, cleaning the bill. His face felt frozen. It took him two minutes before he could get his thoughts back together.

"I feel much better now," he told Inez when he came back out the bathroom.

"Now let me ask you this— how would you feel if all black people was back in Africa?" Inez inquired.

"I think it would be good for everyone. After all, we made this country!" Robo Cop proudly stated.

"Who in the hell told you that!" Inez cursed before she knew it.

"It's a fact," he responded.

"I'm gonna name a few things, tell me if you know what they are: elevator, traffic signals, automatic gearshift, typewriter, fountain pen, advanced printing press, post marking and canceling machine, hard stamp, lawn mower, lawn sprinkler, heating furnace, refrigerator, clothes dryer, home air condition, and supercharger for cars. Do you know about all those things I just named?"

"Yeah, I know what all that is, why?"

"Because all of those things were invented by Black Americans. Now could you say that we are not helpful and very intelligent people?" Inez dropped a major bomb on Robo Cop. He was speechless as he sat there looking dumb.

"I pray God gives you some understanding and your kids don't catch the same disease you got," she stated.

Knock, Knock, Knock,

Both of them looked towards the door. Something just wasn't right. Inez's heart started beating very fast. Feeling it was Kaleem.

"Who is it?" Inez asked.

"Kaleem, Ms. Inez,"

Robo Cop stood up as she opened the door. Kaleem's eyes looked as though he had seen a ghost after he saw Robo Cop face.

"Hi, Kaleem," spoke Ms. Inez.

"Hi," he replied in a soft tone never taken his eyes off Robo Cop.

"My buddy, Kaleem," Robo Cop said. He knew that Ms. Inez wasn't a threat to him plus he cut the phone line to kill the service. Kaleem was hoping that they would leave so Ms. Inez wouldn't stand a chance on getting hurt.

Robo Cop pulled his gun out. "Don't try anything stupid come in and close the door,"

"Oh no! What are you doing?" Ms. Inez yelled.

"Shut up!"

Slap,

He slapped Inez to the floor. Kaleem's reaction made him briefly advance towards Robo Cop until he pointed the gun at him again. Kaleem noticed how big and red Robo Cop eyes were.

"He is high," Kaleem thought. "What the hell do you want?" Kaleem asked.

"Sit down in this chair. Put your hands behind your back." He then taped Kaleem to the chair covering his eyes.

Smack!

Blood sprung from Kaleem's mouth as Robo Cop hit him in his mouth with his gun, chipping his front tooth. "Aww shit!" Kaleem spat. "What the fuck you want?" he asked once again.

"You think this is a game, don't you, Mr. Smart Ass? You hit the streets making all that cash like you don't have a care in the world. Who the fuck, you think you are? You're a black piece of shit that's the only think y'all know how to do. That's why I take all I can from y'all stupid motherfuckers. I want to know where the stash house is and where you keep the money."

"I'm not..."

Slap!

"Wrong answer," Robo Cop hit Kaleem across the side of his face this time.

"Please, God, help us," Ms. Inez cried. "Sir, please stop, please in the name, of God don't hurt him," she reached to grab Robo Cops arm and he slapped her again, knocking her to the floor.

Kaleem was helpless and couldn't see. He could only feel sorry that he had brought this upon the nice old lady that had shown him nothing but the right way to travel in this life. *"Only if I could help her, I know he's gonna kill both of us! God, please forgive me of all my sins. Please be with my mother and family. Lord, my next life I promise to be a much better person."*

"Where's the damn money?" Robo Cop yelled agitated.

The pain from the gun hitting him twice had Kaleem very dizzy. He continued pleading to God, *"Let Queen trust that I meant everything I said to her,"*

"I'm not bullshitting with you man," stated Robo Cop.

Kaleem could hear Inez moaning. He could tell she was getting up off the floor. She was the last person he wanted anything to happen to and it was his entire fault, he thought, *"I should have let Ta'Rod murk his ass like he wanted to and I wouldn't be in this position."*

"That's right," said the Devil.

"Look at what you got us into now. I told you to kill that pig. You knew he was coming after you and Ta'Rod. Don't worry homie you wanted to die anyway falling in love with a woman with AIDS,"

"I'm dying with her in my heart too," Kaleem could hear Robo Cop fumbling inside his pockets. He pulled out his cocaine preparing to inject more cocaine into his nostrils. Kaleem could hear him inhaling the cocaine taking short breaths.

"If Kaleem doesn't give up any information, this time, I am going to blow this nigga's head off. One more off the streets, drug deal gone bad. Like I always said they kill off each other anyway, stupid ass people. All that fighting and shit their ancestors died for in the early years for nothing." The coke had Robo Cop also thinking about what Inez said about his family.

Kaleem's fear circuitry jumped in. He was having flashbacks from when he was a kid, like the Christmas, he got his first bike, and when his mother gave him his first twenty-dollar bill. How he loved his first girlfriend, Tracy back in grammar school. Tracy just never knew she was because she would beat up boys that said they liked her. The smell of death crept through the air. Kaleem's eyes filled up with tears knowing a catastrophe was about to go down. Kaleem said one last prayer, *"Forgive me, Lord..."*

Then the Spirit spoke, *"Why is it that my children can't come begging to me before they hit rock bottom?"*

"You don't look like the man now, Kaleem. Got Internal Affairs on my case. Fuck them! They don't see how I been busting my ass, year after year to see other crooks, thieves, and drug dealers making all the money. That's why I take what I want now. I got this badge as my, do what I want, to who I want to pass! This my last time asking you, where is the fuckin' money house?"

"I told you..."

Robo Cop cut him off. "Wrong answer,"

BOOM! BOOM!

"WHATEVER GOD DOES IS FOR THE BEST!"

To be continued

Epilogue

"Whatever God does is for the best!" Whenever you play the street life, it's always a price to pay. Some pay with their lives or freedom. Families are broken and destroyed.

Santos is sailing on his Yacht that a hood somewhere paid for! Everyone has a relationship with Mr. Devil at times. Don't let his Illusions get you trapped off. His job is to make things look sweet, so you can take the bait.

Every day you must deal with yourself. Kaleem was lost and empty inside, he was just going through the motion until he meets, Queen. Even with her telling him she was infected with the AIDS disease, his heart and soul told him she was his soul mate. His conscience convicted him to take a different route in life. His heart wanted to help keep the younger generation from taken the negative paths in life.

Ta'Rod moved to Kansas and opened up a major club. He is still a part-time pharmacist.

Queen learned not to hate the world she shows that God can use anyone anywhere in life. Even though she carried the AIDS disease, she looked to being supportive and help educate others by being an HIV/AIDS activist. Her heart overtook her beauty.

Every hood has a Robo Cop. He shows the actions of the dirty cops that taxpayers fund, to violate anyone they want too. They need to be monitored on a monthly basis. They are human and their job is imperative and dangerous.

Somewhere in your life, you come across a Ms. Inez, a spiritual person that seen something in you that you may or may not know. Things they may have said that when you had time to stop running you can still hear them now.

Anyone that had been connected to the streets will tell you it's a no win situation. You all are Kings and Queens!

Don't play yourself short. You have the power to change, to be productive in life. To the authors that spread knowledge and wisdom in their writings, many blessings upon all you do. One life saved is priceless!

Speaking of all the adult Queens of 'Brick City' and across the United States, know that you are God's gift to the world.

You are intelligent and beautiful, your morals and values must stand on the qualities of a true woman. You are a powerful source to help build up, the many young girls that have fallen victim to the streets and low self-esteem; By showing, they must seek wisdom, respect, and self-worth. To never settle for less in life. To always, reach for the stars, because they can obtain them.

I challenge you to become a mentor. There is no way they will grow into a woman without knowing what a woman is.

All my Big Dawgs living in 'Brick City' and around the world, yes, you are strong and tough; built to be Kings and Leaders! I challenge all men to take control of your lives and community. We desperately need more mentors willing to help save our Young Black Youth! Black youths face more challenges, especially in low-income homes. They must know they are loved and their lives are of value. Show them how to express their individuality, their self-worth, and self-esteem in positive ways. Explain to them why they should not become a statistic particularly because of the environment they live in.

Become a mentor today, one life saved is priceless!